DO
YOU HEAR
IN THE
MOUNTAINS

. . .

AND OTHER
STORIES

CARAF Books

•

Caribbean and African Literature
Translated from French

RENÉE LARRIER AND MILDRED MORTIMER, *Editors*

DO
YOU HEAR
IN THE
MOUNTAINS

• • •

AND OTHER

STORIES

MAÏSSA BEY

TRANSLATED BY ERIN LAMM

UNIVERSITY OF VIRGINIA PRESS
CHARLOTTESVILLE AND LONDON

This work received support from the French Ministry of Foreign Affairs and the Cultural Services of the French Embassy in the United States through their publishing assistance program.

Entendez-vous dans les montagnes . . . was originally published in French by Éditions de l'Aube, © 2002

Sous le jasmin la nuit was originally published in French by Éditions de l'Aube, © 2004

University of Virginia Press
Translation and Afterword © 2018 by the Rector and Visitors of the University of Virginia
All rights reserved
Printed in the United States of America on acid-free paper

First published 2018

ISBN 978-0-8139-4028-1 (cloth)
ISBN 978-0-8139-4029-8 (paper)
ISBN 978-0-8139-4030-4 (ebook)

9 8 7 6 5 4 3 2 1

Library of Congress Cataloging-in-Publication Data is available for this title.

Cover photo: Kabylie mountains, Algeria. (Shutterstock/Sofilou)

CONTENTS

TRANSLATOR'S ACKNOWLEDGMENTS

To Maïssa Bey, I would like to thank you for the immense privilege of translating and critiquing your work. I would also like to thank you for your support throughout this process. As I wrote to you, the author's approval matters a great deal to me, especially when the work interweaves both rich historic and personal details. Telling another woman's story is a delicate enterprise. I only hope I did *Sous le jasmin la nuit* and *Entendez-vous dans les montagnes . . .* justice and have respected your wishes both as a woman and as an author. I know that part of your father's legacy is the number of women you help to recount their experiences.

As a result of a disability, I use scribes to write. So many hands have touched both texts. So many voices have read them. They also deserve my gratitude. Through *Entendez-vous dans les montagnes . . .* and *Sous le jasmin la nuit,* I learned much about both Algerian and French culture, some of which I was expecting to learn, some unexpected. These are eloquent books, and I did not want to mistranslate them because of a lack of expertise. I hope I have done justice to the Algerian context. Your willingness to teach me has helped in this regard. I also discovered through French and English translation writers—such as the Algerian author Ahlam Mosteghanemi, who explores similar themes to yours in Arabic, including painting a father's portrait for his daughter—the blending of art forms, and the power of artistic expression to reveal and cure emotional and historic questions. In your writing, I see both senses, but an opening to *"coprésences."*

To Odile Cazenave, Dorothy Kelly, Margaret Litvin, and Jeffrey Mehlman, on a professional note, thank you for enriching the translation and critical commentary through your critiques and suggestions. They are much appreciated. The work is much more detailed because of your thoughts. Thank you for agreeing to work with me. I value your flexibility, openness, and attention.

To the late Susan Jackson and family, Dr. Jackson's time and attention to the translation and book proposal was much appreciated. I also valued the time she devoted to me while I was at BU, particularly to my teaching and translation. After my thesis defense, she understood my perspective on Bey's work.

I dedicate my translation of *Entendez-vous dans les montagnes* . . . to my mother and father, with love, and the rest of my family. Like Bey, without my parents' blessing, this book would not have been.

I dedicate my translation of *Sous le jasmin la nuit* to Anaïs and Rose Chabanier, Kalen Valentine, and Kiera Hunter Fisher. Women helping women makes the world a wonderful place.

DO
YOU HEAR
IN THE
MOUNTAINS

• • •

NOVELLA

To him, who will never be able to read these lines

To my sons

Oh, soldiers whose cheek Africa browned
Could you not see that it was mud
Splattering you?

—Victor Hugo, *A l'obéissance passive*
(To passive obedience), 1853

The only picture of Maïssa's father, summer of 1955.

She closes the compartment door behind her in hopes of not being disturbed, of traveling alone. She takes off her coat, carefully folds it, places it close to her. She sits close to the window. She pulls the book begun the night before out of her bag, opens it, and begins to read. The train is almost empty; there is no crowding on the platform. No reserved seats in this compartment. She checked before entering. She lets her reading absorb her bit by bit, only mildly conscious that the train is still at the station.

She jumps at the noise of the door opening softly.

She lifts her eyes.

A man has just come in. He barely casts a glance at her. He ignores her. He closes the door behind him. He takes the seat facing her, close to the window.

He is a man around sixty, in a suit of dark wool, gray shirt with a half-open collar, white hair carefully trimmed and parted, very light-colored eyes, marked features on his face, covered in tracks of delicate craquelures, yet still vigorous.

Why did she have the thought, "he must have been handsome in his youth," as she furtively watched him settle in? Probably because of the sentence she has just read. About this face that just superimposed itself over that of the father, described by the narrator.

"I was observing him with his gray hair and always badly shaven beard, his deeply furrowed brows, the deep lines running from the sides of his nose to the corners of his mouth. I was waiting."

He is not looking at her. Ever since she has been here in this country, she still has difficulty getting used to not existing in others' eyes. A bit as if she has become transparent.

It's as if he were alone in the compartment.

She turns her head to look the other way. Catches their reflection in the window.

He, too, has deeply furrowed brows and bags under his eyes. He seems tired. He will certainly fall asleep as soon as the train leaves the station. Oh she would also like so much to sleep, even if only for a few minutes!

He has only a small, black leather tote that he opens to pull out newspapers, before getting up and putting it in the luggage rack above his seat. Then he sits down again.

Only a few minutes left before departure. The schedules' exactness, still a mystery to her! Departure: 5:48 p.m. Arrival time as listed. Unless there is an unforeseen delay. She is only now beginning to get used to this precise organization of time, and is still astonished that the French complain when you are one minute late.

At the very moment when the train's departure is announced, a young woman opens the door. She glances into the compartment, smiles vaguely, stops for an instant on the threshold, and then decides to come in. There, she sees two people, a woman of a certain age, gazing out the window, who did not even turn her head, and an old, silent gentleman who barely raised his eyes. She will definitely be able to isolate herself . . . With them, the trip will be uneventful, she is sure. She takes off her backpack and settles in next to the man. Right away she pulls her Walkman out of her jacket pocket, puts her earphones into her ears, leans her head back into the crook of the seat, and closes her eyes. She wears a chain around her neck from which the letters of her first name, Marie, hang. She is a young woman with smooth blonde hair, in jeans and sneakers, confident, visibly self-assured, the image of almost all the young women here.

The young woman didn't say hello either. A brief smile, to which no one responded. That's often the way it is. She, the foreign woman, is the only one who finds this abnormal. She will have to get used to it. Rare are those who trouble themselves to look at and greet strangers.

A few minutes ago, the train left the station. She barely noticed. Warehouses have replaced the platforms, and out the window, already, in the coming darkness, buildings move past drowned in fog, then come houses almost identical, with already-lit windows, deserted yards, and dull back courtyards, cluttered with bicycles, folded umbrellas, and abandoned chairs. Groves carefully pruned, ornamental flower beds, hedgerows carefully trimmed and squared, shrubs with pruned foliage, immobile under a metallic sky. Geometric severity. Concern about order. Cutting off everything that overshoots. Disposing of everything bothersome. The sun has long been relegated to behind the clouds.
She closes her eyes.

Maybe another journey or other landscapes fill her head.

Behind her lowered eyelids stretches of pebbly, dust-covered landscapes move, ceaselessly windswept. Then forests, some underbrush, some paths invaded by brambles. And, every once in a while, in the wastelands on the outskirts of cities and villages, little stacks of white or gray stones resembling unnatural growths are piled carelessly to delineate graves, filling the cemeteries having neither fences nor hedges in her homeland's countryside. With splashes of red. Red, the color of wild geraniums that grow and bloom on the burial mounds, without anyone ever being able to know who planted them. Here and there, only a few scrawny old abandoned trees, randomly dispersed at the whim of a miserly nature, too frugal with her favors. Rare are those that give shade. The skies back there are almost always cloudless.

This may be the end of a long somnolence. Why now, as he looks at this silent woman's face, leaning against the window and seeming aloof from everything happening around her, why are those men's voices ringing in his ears, with a frightening shrillness?

She has her eyes closed.

He had the time, in a brief flash, to see her eyes without meeting her gaze.

In those dark eyes and that evasive gaze turned toward the night, suddenly form the shadowy reflections of distant nights jumbling together in a clamor of shouts and supplications.

The outstretched hands of these men, who no longer believe, who no longer trust in mankind.

Yet, the taste for the sun still remains with him. A blaze, like an unbearable acuity, giving to men, to all men, a dark stare. Yes, that is it. Obsession with the sun beating in that vein in his temples, making them ache. Which today darkens the contours of his memories. Even through closed eyes. Even in sleep's illusory void. Even in the vain confusions and ramblings of drunkenness. Even in silence's throbbing echoes.

Pounding.

One! Two! March!

Their feet sink into dust. Into mud, at times. Crusted mud weighing down their pataugas. *Smudging the back of their pants.*

March!

"We are the Africans who come back from afar . . ."† *Snippets of songs stuck like burrs in the innermost recesses of consciousness.*

Let's go! All together! Louder! I can't hear you!

"We comin' from the colonies to defend our country . . ."

Men stumble over loose rubble. They get stuck in the un-

---

* Traditional Basque linen shoes.—*Trans.*

† From the World War I–era song "Le chant des Africains," which suggested it was an African's duty to fight for France; used by the *pieds-noirs* during the Algerian War of Independence to justify maintaining the French presence in Algeria.—*Trans.*

derbrush. Trekking. Roundups. By day or by night. Keep your nerve! Keep your nerve! Company . . . forward, march!*

"Do you hear . . . in the countryside, roa-a-a-ar these ferocious soldiers . . ."*

Yes, fierce. Bloodthirsty. Their dark stare. Rage in their eyes. Even shut. Even bloodshot. Even in the final instant preceding death.

On the ground, puddles of blood, urine and shit, mixed with splashes of soapy water that they can no longer swallow. The funnel fills up and sloshes over the edge without being able to empty inside their stomachs, immeasurably bloated beyond recognition. Bitter smell of blood and vomit . . . sometimes of burned flesh.

Sometimes the neon lights flicker, almost going out, and their faces are streaked by flashes from the lights outside.

Maybe it's the screech of the wheels on the rails each time the train, thrust into high velocity, slows. And in the wake of this train traveling through the peaceful night, slowly rises *the noise of the gégène,*† *the crank that a man's hand had to turn, or that had to be turned on with a pedal, like one of those country telephones—a constant noise, a creaking similar to the creak of a well's pulley. At times covered by long howls that die in moans and resonate for a long time in the night.*

She does not feel very well. The train's screech from time to time as it slows sets her teeth on edge, as would an acidic taste. Maybe it is also because of what she just read. Given what this book talks about that she chose by accident while going

---

* "Roundups" (*ratissages*) were common in both France and Algeria during the Algerian War of Independence. Purportedly to prevent suspected terrorists from interacting with civilians, they could target anyone who looked even vaguely Algerian. Algerians were known in French slang as *"ratons,"* or "baby rats." — *Trans.*

† Composed of a crank and dynamo, the *gégène* was the machine most typically used for torture in Algeria, and could be powered by telephone lines.—*Trans.*

through a bookstore, no, not really by accident, but based on a few passages read while flipping through it, questions asked by this man who is interrogating his father to understand the past.

She lets her thoughts wander . . . not very far, while rereading the answers . . . Due to an accidental encounter, an answer to a question which is not even clearly posed.

"No, I'm not talking about received orders and obedience. The executioner doesn't obey orders. He does his job. He doesn't hate those whom he executes, he doesn't take revenge on them, he doesn't eliminate them because they are bothersome to him or threatening towards him or aggressive towards him. He is completely indifferent to them."

One question, the same one, always, comes to mind while the man across from her looks for his glasses in his jacket pocket, before unfolding a newspaper.

How old must he be? Over sixty, that's for sure . . .

This obsession . . . the question she often asks when she finds herself facing men of that age, a question she always attempts to suppress.

Those wrinkles etched like stigmata at the corners of his lips. My father would be nearly the same age. No, he would be even older. He would not look like that . . . he was much shorter . . . maybe he would have ended up looking like his father . . .

The conditional comes automatically in the sentences that just sprang into her mind, even as she drifts off into a light doze.

She often tried to re-create her father's face. Fragment by fragment. Still, she only knows of him what she looks at again and again in pictures. A younger man, content, smiling into the camera lens. All of these memories crystallize around the sparkle of his glasses, behind which his smiling or serious eyes seem small. No, nothing, nothing about his voice, nor his smell, nor his stride, she remembers nothing. Still, certain words are present, bits of sentences that still linger in her memory. But not the sound of his voice. Not the tone he used when speaking to her. Other very brief images: her father standing in front of his classroom door, in his gray teacher's uniform, then in shirt-sleeves, sitting in an armchair on the terrace, totally relaxed, his face offered to the sun, or standing alone, with his back against the schoolyard wall during recess.

She never understood how and why his glasses remained intact. They were the only "personal effects" that they were able to recover, with his wedding ring that someone—but who?—had taken off his finger.

The man laid his hand on the narrow window sill. A very white hand with brown spots, crisscrossed by very apparent veins, gnarled fingers, closely clipped and ribbed nails. An old man's hand, still and withheld, with a finely wrought white gold wedding band on his ring finger.

From time to time, he casts a curious glance at her. An inquisitive gaze. As if he was searching for something in her face.

She does not like trains with compartments. She does not like overnight trains. Fear is there, present, beating in her stomach; it has not left her for years, so present that it has become a familiar companion for her that she still cannot manage to tame. What is she afraid of in this train that is taking her toward the Old Port City?* This train is going to the sea. That should make her a little happier. There, she will again find the light of days, the smell and the tumult of the sea. At least that.

The man suddenly turns to look at the young woman sitting near him. He stares at her with a smile that abruptly softens his features.

The young woman with the Walkman has fallen asleep, her mouth open. Relaxed, confident. Of whom, or what, would she, Marie, be afraid?

She cannot fall asleep. Half-consciously, she lets herself be rocked gently by the even cadence of the advancing machine.

A slight jolt. The train just pulled into a station. Stopped for

* Marseilles. — *Trans.*

three minutes. Passengers get off. Others get on, no noise, no bustle. Then, again, the streets of the city slowly crossed. Her face flattened against the window, she looks out.

So this is France.

These men and women free, so free, so different . . .

Women's confident gestures as they walk down the street at a brisk pace, heads held high, looking straight ahead. The sparkle of lights from shops' display windows, the rain, the puddles that reflect lights turned on sometimes in broad daylight. Men and women always in a hurry, the very particular odor of the subway, the heat of this breath traveling through the underground tunnels, bearing dust and gloom. Walls covered in graffiti, colors and shapes of letters tightly nestled as if to mask the concrete in powder makeup. Posters, everywhere, nude bodies, given, entwined, in unseemly embraces. And all of these couples holding each other so close, the need they have to touch each other, to caress each other, and to kiss each other, everywhere, anywhere, as if seized at every moment by an imperious need to assure themselves that they really belong to one another. Sweet France*. . .

Deep in thought, gently rocked by the train's cadence, she ends up barely . . . dozing off.

She is abruptly wrested from her doze, by shouts, shrieking voices, and calls. She starts, sitting up straight, worried. She gazes at the man, who does not move, as if he had heard nothing. He has his eyes fixed on his newspaper. The young woman wakes up. She still has her earphones in her ears. Without rising, she looks at the closed door, as if she expected to see someone come in. People run in the hallway. And, with a loud screech of wheels, the train brakes then stops. At that instant, the man lifts his eyes. He leans over, looks out the window, and turns to look her way.

He must be slightly deaf, she thinks. He almost did not react.

---

* "Douce France" ("Sweet France") was a popular song recorded in 1947 that evokes nostalgic, traditional images of France. — *Trans.*

She doubtless has a strange expression on her face, because
he looks at her astonished:

"Aren't you feeling well?"

She shakes her head:

"No . . . it's fine, it's this noise."

Her voice is hoarse, as if she had a sore throat. She has not
spoken for a long time.

Behind the door, running can still be heard, then the door
opens.

A woman bursts into the compartment. She steps forward
then backward, stopping on the threshold. She seems beside
herself. First she looks at them, without saying anything. The
young woman now sits up straight.

Something really abnormal is happening. Shouts are heard,
then whistles blow. Doors open or close again violently. People
call to each other.

She looks out the window. Total darkness. They are stopped
in the middle of fields. She sees nothing except her own
reflection.

The woman ends up coming in and remains standing in the
middle of the compartment. She breathes noisily and splutters
in one breath:

"Thugs! Thieves! They got on the train . . . they tried to attack passengers who were sleeping in the first-class cars."

The young woman takes her earphones out of her ears. She
gets up.

"What happened?"

The woman repeats:

"Thugs . . . on the train! They tried to attack passengers
in the next car. Haven't you seen anything?"

The teenager does not seem very impressed. She goes toward
the door and takes a few steps in the visibly deserted hallway.

The woman clasps her hand to her heart; she has difficulty
catching her breath.

"I was asleep, but I heard them . . . I was sleeping with
one eye open. With everything that's happening, one just never
knows. And then, all of a sudden, everyone started shouting.

Fortunately! They were on the run! I saw them go right in front of me . . . Arabs, I'm sure! I saw them! We should not open the doors now, they have to be arrested! They have to be arrested! They really have to . . . they really have to be caught! Oh my God! I've never been so scared!"

Her voice is sharp, speaking very fast, she again repeats:

"I saw them . . . they should not be allowed to escape . . . they . . . they should be arrested! They shouldn't get out of this one! All the same, it's unbelievable! We can't even travel in peace anymore . . . I hope the doors haven't been opened!"

The train is still stopped but no one can hear anything anymore.

Right now, the woman is standing in the doorway. She hugs her bag very tightly to her chest. She turns her back to them, looks into the hall, to the right and to the left, shakes her head nervously, on pins and needles. Then she blurts out:

"My suitcase! My suitcase!"

She dashes into the hallway.

The man looks at the woman seated facing him. He has an embarrassed smile on his lips, as if he wanted to excuse what was just said.

He knows, he understood.

The young woman comes back. She tells them evenly:

"I don't see anything. Everything's calm! Maybe it was just . . . a simple scuffle."

She goes back to her seat, sits down with her legs curled underneath her, and turns to the woman sitting facing her.

"You let your book drop, madame."

The man leans over, picks it up and holds it out to her, not without having cast a glance at the title, *The Reader,* by Schlink.

He nods his head. In a barely audible voice, she thanks him, without even looking at him.

That's the way it is . . . it always has to be that way.

How can this woman be sure that they are Arabs? A rapid

glance in the semi-darkness of the train was enough for her. Obviously, as soon as there is a theft, a fight, an assault, it could only be them. No need to look further. She tries to convince herself that they were not Algerians . . . as if that could change anything.

She takes her head in her hands pressing very hard against her forehead, as if to eradicate all the thoughts she could no longer manage to put in order. She truly feels sick. She can no longer bear any allusion to violence, and now she finds herself caught up again by everything she has been attempting in vain to flee.

He rises, comes up to her, bends over:

"I am a doctor. Maybe I could . . ."

She shakes her head.

"No, no, I'm fine . . ."

He is very close to her. She detects his scent. A scent she recognizes. A very subtle fragrance. She turns her head once more to look away.

"It's nothing . . . just a passing dizzy spell. I'm used to it . . . it's going to pass very soon, don't worry!"

He keeps looking at her. This attention, this insistent gaze fixed on her, unsettles her. She would like to get up, to go out into the hallway, or rather to take her suitcase and get off the train that just started again very slowly at that same instant. She plans a move and then lets herself fall back onto the seat. What for? Where could she go?

"Are you sure that . . ."

She raises her head again, forces herself to smile.

"I was only a little . . . dizzy, only a bit lightheaded. This often happens to me. It's okay, there, it's passing, it's better now!"

He insists:

"Maybe you need a very strong coffee with a lot of sugar. Would you like a . . ."

"No, no, I assure you there's no need, I don't want to trouble you, everything is fine."

She leans her head against the back of the seat, then closes her eyes, troubled by that look that seems to express more than simple solicitude . . . a real desire to come to her aid.

The man sat back down. He took up his newspaper again, but he does not seem very focused on his reading. He lifts his eyes from time to time in order to observe her.

It was only a dizzy spell. She doesn't feel anything anymore but an immense distress, and especially a desire to arrive at her destination very quickly. She still has to spend several hours here, in this car. No! She has to get ahold of herself. It is going to be alright. She is eager for this trip to finally end. All of these departures, all of these stops . . . When will she be able to settle down, to breathe a little? She does not understand what is happening to her. In the past, she has always been resilient. It is certainly the fatigue built up over the last few days, the tension of the last few months . . . an emotionalism burgeoning on the surface of her skin, a sensitivity that she did not recognize within herself. To flee . . . to leave everything behind without looking back, to try to find a link, a friend, a place to hole up . . . to reconnect with the ones who came here before her, who have already been here for a few years. How did *they* manage? How were they able to get acclimated? She is unable to get used to the idea that she will doubtless be here for a long time. Yes, this could be a temporary residency . . . indefinitely extended. She has not really felt well since she has been here. She feels as if the earth, which carries her, is moving under her feet. For several weeks, she has been attempting to keep herself balanced in order to move forward . . . putting one foot in front of the other; that appears simple. Her head is heavy . . . so heavy from the effort of rehashing all of these thoughts. She feels exhausted, breathless, right now . . . suddenly, as if she had made a great effort.

He is in midsentence. However, entirely absorbed in this weakness that she cannot quite overcome, she does not listen; then, she catches words, a sentence that makes her pay attention:

"I'm a doctor, but . . . I have not been practicing for some time. I know your country well."

Her country? How did he know? Of course, it jumps out at you, especially since . . . but I could have been . . . maybe it's the silver earrings . . . for someone who knows the country well, Kabyle jewelry is readily identifiable . . . but that's it, that's also why she wears them, yes, to never forget who she is, and especially to make sure others don't forget what she is, a foreign woman, that's all.

As if he had heard her pronounce those words, he pointed to her suitcase above her in the luggage rack.

"Right there . . . your suitcase."

She raises her head and looks. Her address back there, her only real address, is still written on the tag hanging from the handle of her suitcase. Pretty visible. Her name too. He knows my name, where I come from, maybe even . . . and yes, that I am just passing through . . .

He repeats, in a quavering voice:

"It's just that . . . I knew Algeria well."

That's quite often how discussions begin here, as soon as they learn that she is Algerian. A few years ago, during her first stay in France, upon her arrival, the customs agent who screened her was a Frenchman born in her village, one of the repatriated. Such a tremendous coincidence that she remained speechless for a long while. She did not even know what to respond when he rattled off the names of students who had been with him at the high school, names that were all familiar to her. She had to promise to give a telephone number to one of her neighbors, who happened to be one of the classmates of the tireless customs agent, with such a vivid memory, so moved to have news from the country. He bombarded her with questions about everything: the streets, the houses, the town square, the newspaper stand, the school . . . and about everyone: from the former cleaning woman, a little maid who must be pretty old by now, to the Mozabite corner grocer, before letting her leave with visibly heartfelt reluctance.

And then . . . there is also the particular curiosity of all those who sympathize . . .

"How is it back there?" With pitying or worried expressions. And right away, they inevitably add: "With everything that's going on . . ." Some even talk about "the events in Algeria,"* a venerated expression, as in the past. She expects the question now. He is going to say those words, he is going to say them, that's for sure.

Yet he seems to be elsewhere, he does not want to talk anymore. Fortunately. She doesn't either.

She could have thanked him anyway for his solicitude, he is going to take her for a . . .

"Thank you . . . thank you."

She has not stopped thanking everyone ever since she has been here. Thank you for understanding, your support, your often sincere desire to come to my aid or the way you elegantly shut the doors in my face, softly, thank you for your pity, your sometimes perfidious interest, thanks to the sympathetic ones, who ask questions about "what's going on," so many questions that I do not know how to, I cannot answer, because they are the same questions I ask myself.

Defensively shielded, she wears her difference like a piece of armor. She is not from here.

She lets herself be carried from exile to exile; first over there, a foreigner in her own country because she refused to abdicate, to let herself be swept away by this enormous wave that submerged one after another so many men and women. She does not know, no she does not know which shoreline she should hail to finally feel free from this solidly anchored anguish that has pursued her all the way here. She doesn't want to, she no longer wants to talk about what she has left behind: her house, her job, her daily routine. Not to think about her loved ones, about the sun, about the light and about the smell of the days, about this intolerable suffering around her such as . . .

Weary, she lets herself go back into the seat.

* "Events" was the euphemism used to refer to the struggle for independence in Algeria before the struggle was formally named. — *Trans.*

"You're . . ."

She interrupts him:

"Yes. Algerian, that's it."

This said without smiling.

"That's not what I meant . . ."

To put an end to the questions, the explanations, she adds: "I live here now."

Why did she specify "now"? I am not an emigrant, that's what she meant. But what difference does that make, especially in their eyes? I am an exile, nothing more. Or rather a refugee. I have the right to temporary residency, it's written on my passport. During the time that . . .

"I have a lot of trouble picturing what's happening over there."

There it is. Of course, how could he? She too, for a few years, has had a lot of trouble opening her eyes to the reality each morning. Even here. She didn't come looking to forget. Only for a respite. But how could she, when all they bring up is her country's bloody front?

"Such a beautiful country . . ."

What country is he talking about? That nostalgia in his voice. No, much more than nostalgia, suffering, something stemming from his face, in his eyes, his way of averting his eyes, of pronouncing his words without looking at her.

"I remember it . . . I remember it very well . . . It was . . . It was . . . a long time ago, a very long time ago."

She looks at him, a little surprised by the slight crack she just detected in his voice. That's what they always say about Algeria: what a beautiful country! With an exclamation point and of course, a verb in the past tense, even if it is implicit! She has heard this sentence everywhere, for such a long time, said in a tone of regret during the first few years that followed independence, but now tinged with commiseration. Yes, the beaches, the desert, the hot sand, the sun, the light . . .

Still, in this country, there are men. In every country, there are men. It is they who make it into a homeland. Who make it into a hell. Or a country that's nice to live in.

His Algeria: these are certainly the beaches of Fort de l'Eau and La Madrague, the rounds of anisette at evening fall, the odor of *kémia,* of *mouna,* and of *merguez*ˢ kebabs, tanning sessions with feet dangling in the water, rounds of *pétanque* in the paths of Bab el Oued Park, the Saturday-night dances in the village squares, spins around the Ruisseau des singes, fairs, open-air bars . . . happiness . . . lost happiness . . . nostalgia, that is certainly what he means.

"I spent eighteen months there, I was drafted."

The privates walk down the trail, their necks crushed under a leaden sun. The weight of the rifle on their shoulders, the grenades on their belts. They have sore feet, backs in shreds, eyes irritated by sweat. They are racked with fear. Behind every bush, they conjure up an enemy, in ambush, ready to spring and slit their throats. They were warned. They are fierce, blood-thirsty. They were shown photos as soon as they got to the barracks. The little guy from the squad, with his throat slit, his testicles in his mouth. He will never forget. And those who never came back . . . The list is long. Medals and citations. Died for France. Killed in their prime on the field of honor. Their names are engraved in the squares of the villages of France. Heroes dead in defense of their homeland. Which homeland? Their fathers' land?

. . . And what could be said of the others?

One morning, Bernard is missing from roll call. Gone AWOL. During the night, he joined the maquis, the fellouzes over there in the djebels,⁺ taking arms and munitions with him. He crossed the line. Without saying anything to anyone. As for Jean, he stayed in the barracks. More alone than ever. All those

---

ˢ *Kémia, mouna,* and *merguez* are, respectively, green olives, a type of brioche, and a spicy sausage. —*Trans.*

⁺ *Maquis (maquisards)* were resistance fighters. The term was used during the Algerian War for Independence and then again during the civil war of the 1990s, the "Black Decade." *"Fellouze"* is highly pejorative, related to *"fellaga,"* a common insult used to refer to an Algerian resistance fighter. The *djebels* are mountains. —*Trans.*

nights spent talking ceaselessly, trying to understand, to tame the horror. In vain. Bernard ended up choosing the other camp. No one ever saw him again.

Jean never saw the others either . . . the ones who, like him, came back . . .

But does one ever come back from there?

She says nothing. Why does he want to talk about Algeria? Simply because she is Algerian? That's not really a rare breed around here. She has nothing to say, nothing to say to him. She picks up her book again.

A sentence jumps out at her:

"When he spoke, he gave me a lecture on the person, liberty and dignity, on a human being as subject and on the fact that we don't have the right to treat a human as an object."

Such a beautiful country! Bled out at present. Victim of too many celebrations or cursed by the gods, residing there regardless of the season—not only in the spring.

Of course, the days are still bathed in sunlight, but the nights are presently haunted by deeper and deeper shadows, as if allowing men to give free reign to their inner demons. And, night and day, doors are shut, bolted over the stunned silence that has fallen upon beings, a silence charged with immeasurable anguish that liquidates the echoes of shouts and calls that remain unanswered.

She fled under threat. She left that country in order to come find refuge here. What an irony of history! She, the daughter of "a glorious martyr of the revolution," of a man executed for having wanted to chase France out of his country, here she is, seeking refuge among those whom he, the teacher, the hero honored today during so many commemorations and whose name the village's school bears, had fought!

She no longer wants to bear the shock of daily executions, massacres and accounts of massacres, landscapes disfigured by terror, innumerable funeral processions, mothers' howls . . . menacing stares . . . She fled to attempt to protect herself from shattering, petrifying, crushing fear, and especially what ends up diverting you from all human feeling, because it blinds to the point of giving birth to rage, violence, the irrepressible desire for vengeance, the temptation to kill before being killed . . .

She fled. And now, she definitely does not want anyone to speak to her about her country. Neither in the past, nor in the present.

She looks at him without saying a word. But he does not expect a response. He continues, as if he were talking to himself.

"Yes . . . I spent several months there, first working in an office and then as a medical aide, in an infirmary. In a military camp. A special camp. And then . . ."

The camp is surrounded by walls topped with barbed wire and guard towers. The men that they bring here day and night, cuffed or already nastily battered, are fearsome terrorists. In any case, all terrorists are fearsome . . . The zone is particularly dangerous. Not only because of the site's layout . . . Captain Fleury hammers home: you have to know, here, there are no suspects. There are only the guilty. Guilty of remaining silent, of opening their door to fellagas, of furnishing them with provisions, of giving them money, by choice or by force, it doesn't matter, and of informing for them. They know how to make them talk . . . You hear? All . . . they are all accomplices! You have to make them talk whatever the cost! Otherwise, you are the ones we're going to find on the roadside, ratted out by these bastards, with your balls torn off! Get that through your thick skulls!

He pauses for an instant. Then he takes up the charge again: "Do you live in Algiers?"

She nods her head. He did not use the past tense. Yet . . .

She corrects, mechanically:

"Yes, Algiers . . . well . . . I used to live in Algiers."

"And . . . do you know Boghari? A village near the Portes du Sud. Not very far from Algiers. Well . . . not really a village . . . rather a large market town."

She starts, out of breath. She cannot help but clench her fists very tightly, so tightly that her nails bite deeply into her palm, and finally, pain forces her to react.

He seems not to have noticed anything.

No, no . . . she will ask no questions.

She was born in Boghari. She lived there. Until her father's death.

He did not notice the pallor that invaded her face. He feels like talking. For the first time. The first time since . . . He stares at a spot behind her as if he were staring at a screen, and continues in a low voice.

Why does he want to talk? He does not know. He does not know if she is listening. It makes little difference to him. He repeats one more time:

"I'm a doctor. I finished school after the war. Over there, I was stationed at the camp infirmary. Occasionally . . . I really believed that they needed medics to take care of men . . ."

He resumes slowly:

"Men . . . It's true; at times I happened to take care of them . . ."

He has not noticed anything, entirely engrossed in his memories. She is suddenly cold . . . very cold. A breath of icy wind has just engulfed her that makes her shiver from head to foot.

She often pictured THE scene. But for as long as she has been here, paradoxically, she ended up not thinking about it anymore. Probably because other scenes, real enough, have come to supplant the images she was trying to manufacture from other accounts. From other scenes described by those who had survived. Even as a little girl, she tried to put a face on the men who had tortured and finished off her father before throwing him into a mass grave. But she could not manage to give them a man's face. They could only be monsters . . . like the ones who today, for other reasons and in almost the same places, are slitting children's, women's, and men's throats. She then saw men in balaclavas, clothed entirely in black in order to better fade into the night, a little bit like the images of executioners portrayed in history books and films. Faceless men who had long haunted her dreams. Later, fortified by her certainties, she added: men who had nothing human about them.

She does not want to, she does not want to hear any more about it. And what if she got up now? What if she went out, changed compartments, got off at the next station? What if she asked him softly, but firmly, to be quiet? She would very much like to be able to say . . . excuse me, I have a headache . . . all the more since she feels a real physical malaise that she just became conscious of. Her head is caught in a vise and painful stabs gouge her temples.

As if looking for a means to stem the suffering that has just reemerged, she looks to the young woman, who, seeing them speaking, took her earphones out a little while ago, certainly to take part in the conversation.

"I have a lot of Algerian friends. Really . . . they all say it's a very beautiful country. My grandfather too. He talks about it all the time. He was born over there."

And there! We've come full circle! A *pied-noir*'s grand-daughter, a veteran, a *fellaga*'s daughter.[*] It's almost unreal. Really, who could have imagined such a scene? It looks like a television studio, gathered for a show by journalists in search of truth, hoping to lift the veil to shed light on *"France's painful past."* All that is missing is a *harki.*[†] And especially, to empha-size this situation's absurdity and strangeness, they should not neglect to introduce her not only as a *fellaga*'s daughter, but as herself obliged to flee her country to escape the fundamentalist madness. Someone could even write a play about it and choose

---

[*] A *pied-noir* is someone of typically French origin in Algeria who sup-ported French rule (*"noir"* referring to soldiers' black boots); *fellaga* is a derogatory term for an Algerian resistance fighter. — *Trans.*

[†] An Algerian who collaborated and fought with the French army during the Algerian War for Independence. — *Trans.*

an intentionally commonplace title, for example: "Conversation in a Train." Act I. Characters in place.

Strangely, she hears her double say:

"I . . . I know Boghari well. I was born there . . ."

Encouraged by this answer, the man seems to feel like continuing his impressions. He runs his hand through his hair several times, leans toward her, and resumes more firmly:

"I did all of my basic training there. There were large barracks, seven kilometers from the village, in the mountains. It was called . . . Boghar. It was . . . the end of 1956, beginning of 1957, during the events. Things happened over there . . . Strolls in the vicinity were not highly recommended . . ."

He stops for an instant, then, as if to make her act as a witness, he turns sharply toward the young woman, who is also listening to him.

"But . . . it was a very beautiful region . . . if . . ."

She feels her heart beating a little faster. Her hands are icy. The date . . . She does not dare to take full stock of what is actually happening at this instant. And there is that "if" . . . followed by a silence. Why is he hesitating? She would like him to . . . no, she doesn't know if she really wants to let him keep talking, without telling him anything. But the conversation has now begun.

"I don't know if it's still like that. There were trees, a lot of trees in the region. A magnificent forest . . . pines and larches, I think. Then . . . winding paths . . . and a terrible cold in winter! Never, I would have never ever thought that it could be that cold over there! They didn't prepare us for that. We patrolled all over, it seemed like everywhere. Do you know the region well?"

"A little . . . a few vague memories. My father took us there sometimes in the car on Sundays."

Her voice trembles. She is not sure he heard her.

She does not really remember much about the region, its beauty. She was too young. She does not know if it is still "so nice." These last years, many forests have been burned because they served as havens for terrorist groups, many trees on the roadsides were also cut down to prevent ambushes. She remembers only having read in a newspaper, not so long ago, that the barracks at Boghar were attacked one night, by armed groups presented by certain foreign journalists as *"presumed"* Islamic fundamentalists. A bloodbath. All the victims were young men drafted for military service. A frightening number of deaths. At that time, she had asked her mother if it was really there that they would stroll in the past, trying to remember the Sunday outings from her childhood. She remembers only the feeling of nausea that overwhelmed her every time they had to go up there in the car. She was nervous about the trip because of the windy narrow road, a real torture.

It's like opening the floodgates to let muck flow out, all the mire from a past that appears very close and still sensitive. Like running your finger over or touching an old scar the edges of which had scabbed over, or so you thought, you felt a slight ooze, which was transformed bit by bit into pus, which ends up flowing more and more abundantly, without your being able to stop it.

"You were young, certainly too young . . . you can't remember all of that, of course."

You'd almost think that he is looking to . . . to reassure himself. Should she now tell him her age? Or talk to him about places from her childhood?

She is not looking to correct him, to tell him that if she doesn't remember the trees, the beauty of the region, she remembers all the rest.

The young woman moved closer. Without really grasping what is going on between this man and this woman seeming to be peacefully discussing, in search of common memories, she is listening; she wants to be told about this country that she does not know but that is part of her family history.

And she's the one the woman wants to speak to. She turns toward her:

"And you? Haven't you ever been there?"

Marie shakes her head:

"No, no. My parents were born here. My grandfather . . . he's my grandfather on my mother's side . . . he left Algeria in . . . I don't know when, after the war, like all the other French. He never set foot there again. But he talks about it all the time. He still has his photos . . . a bunch of photos that he never stops taking out when we come. I would have very much liked to . . ."

The man interrupts:

"Maybe it is not the best time to go there!"

He pronounces these words drily. It is more of a warning than a piece of advice.

The woman feels hurt. She feels the reproach in his voice, a reproach that he addresses to her, as if he did not approve of her question, or . . . yes, it seems rather that he wants to get to her, to hurt her.

What he wants to tell her and what he does not dare to, perhaps because she, the foreign woman, *is* there, is certainly this: No, little Marie with such clear eyes and such blonde curls, it's not the time to go over there . . . especially not you. There is no reason to put your life in danger. As far as tourism goes, there are many other countries to discover. Countries where you can walk in the streets and tan in the sun without fear of being singled out and slaughtered. Some calmer countries, some more . . . orderly people, where they know how to properly welcome tourists in search of folklore, a change of scenery, and exoticism. Did you know that that one is listed among the ten most dangerous countries on the planet? Very dangerous, even and especially for those who live there! And if you're really set on going, you will still need to wait a long time before discovering this country that is beautiful, in the end, only in the memory of those who left it!

Mission accomplished. They just left the small hamlet nestled in the hollow of a valley. What they call here a mechta.

Or rather what remains of it. A few clouds of smoke rise over houses. Or rather what remains of them. The guys in the chopper did a good job. The planes returned to base. Everything is silent around them now. A silence that rings in their ears and seems still to resonate with the moans of those they left behind. The lieutenant gave the order to slaughter the dog whose howls would be the death of them ever since they went in. Jean gets his rifle ready. The dog hiding behind a bush scented danger. He bolts yapping and zigzagging. Jean lowers his weapon. They all burst out laughing.*

The conversation must continue, and especially, must go back to the past, whatever the cost. It is too easy to pity oneself because of the present. To get out of the game unscathed.

At the moment when the woman opens her mouth to answer, the teenager resumes, not at all impressed by the warning:

"I know, of course, I know. But because I've heard my friends . . . and my grandfather talk about it so much, I really want to go there . . ."

"Why not? As soon as possible, I will go back there, too."

The woman has just spoken, very calmly, herself astonished by the brisk determination with which she affirmed what now seems obvious to her. Of course, she will go back to her home, and earlier than she had until then thought; she is certain of it.

And since he evoked Boghari, Boghar, since he has given dates, he must talk right away. He has to see it through. She also has to see it through to the bitter end. Nothing seems more important to her at this instant.

She addresses him conversationally:

"And you, haven't you been back there since . . . ?"

"No, never."

"You could have . . . in wartime you cannot discover all of a country's beauties."

"I know. But what I saw of . . ."

---

* A reference to a particular kind of torture, in which people were threatened with being thrown out of a helicopter; some who refused to talk were actually thrown out. — *Trans.*

It is now the young woman, who resumes:
"You were in the war? Over there?"
"I was twenty . . . fit to serve."
"And . . ."

Twenty years old, sometimes less, sometimes a little more. Blond hair cropped by the barrack's barber, from induction, even before departure, watch out, it's infested with lice over there, with crabs too, eyes reddened by apprehension, yes, his tender heart still shaken up by the vision of a mother in tears on the dock, the memory of a distraught fiancée, waving her handkerchief, and then the photos so as not to forget, photos sorted the night before, in his fatigues pocket all the time, right against his heart . . . this woman's face that he looks at every night before going to sleep, or the child's with chubby cheeks, with blue eyes, blond hair, as light as a feather, the very portrait of his father . . . how he misses those pudgy little arms around his neck, the warm breath against his cheek, the odor of innocence . . .

Marie waits for the rest. The man, who never finishes his sentences, has turned his head away; he looks out the window. He sees nothing but a procession of far-off lights rushing past in the night. Around them are deep shadows.

Suddenly, with a slightly stiff smile, he interrogates:
"So they talked to you about . . . about the war, about the Algerian War?"

"Of course. My grandfather talked to me about it . . . but . . . he, he says 'the events . . .' and I often feel like he doesn't really like when we ask him questions. He says that it was very hard, yes . . . and . . . he doesn't really like talking about it. But he . . . he lived in a village. He was a primary school teacher. He never had problems with the . . ."

She stops suddenly and bites her lips.

That's right, how to say it? The Arabs? But surely after the way in which this word was just pronounced in this very spot by a woman traumatized by a scuffle, a purely *French* woman without any doubt, it is difficult not to see hints of racism. But after all, we've always needed classifications for living species, animal as well as human. So why not designate men by their race? Or by their religion, even if many of them have grown distant from it? They say "the Jews" too. They can vary this by specifying one's belonging to a people, a human classification, a region, a tribe. You have to have points of reference in order to be able to situate someone! Why would this be insulting? Would the insult be contained in the word, or only in the intention, or even in the representation that we have of the race, of the group thus designated? How many words, expressions must have been invented for them! Depending on historical context. All sorts of figures of speech, of compound expressions, a profusion of words: natives, Muslim Frenchmen from Algeria, wogs, *bougnoules, métèques, melons,** *moukères, Fatma*† for women, all women, North African or even better, to mark the strides of official colonial vocabulary: Pure-bred French of North African origin . . . PFNAO for short. All of these terms are duly inventoried at length in dictionaries, with, for certain ones, a necessary clarification: insulting, racist terms. For Arabs, the French—and by extension all Europeans—are *roumis,* which, from a historical, etymological, and in a certain way . . . objective point of view, simply recalls that at one time in their history, they were subjects of Rome.

The young woman blushed slightly. In order to come to her aid, the woman finishes the sentence smiling:

"With the Arabs you mean . . ."

She continues in the same detached fashion:

"My father was a primary school teacher, too."

"Oh, really? That's unbelievable! And in the same country! Maybe they . . . It's really too bad, I don't know the name of the village where my grandfather lived. I only know that it was

---

*Pejorative terms of various origins referring to Algerians or those from the Maghreb, often aimed at immigrants.—*Trans.*

† *Moukères* comes from the Spanish *mujer,* a slang term for a woman. *Fatma* is a stereotypical name for a Maghrebi or, more generally, African woman.—*Trans.*

at the shore. He was crazy about fishing. As a matter of fact, he still fishes for days on end . . . up to now . . . he lives in Marseilles. Ever since he retired, *that's* all he ever does . . . but it's been such a long time . . . your father is . . ."

"He is dead."

"Oh, excuse me! I am . . ."

Yes . . . she is . . . sorry. That is what is said in such circumstances.

She continues to look at her smiling as if to tell her, no, you have no part in this, little Marie. You don't have to be sorry. *You* have nothing to do with it!

He's doomed. There is nothing more to get out of him. Take him away! Two of them pull the inert man's body lying on the ground. All the same, he lasted a long time, says the lieutenant with a kind of admiration. He's a hard-ass! Well . . . he was . . . Cleanup duty now. Let the others finish the job! Day is just beginning to break. With a heavy step, they come back up to the surface. Outside, the air is fresh. Pink clouds scatter what remains of the night. Jean fills his lungs with air before lighting a cigarette. The first of the day. Or rather the last of the night. It is time to go to sleep. He stretches, with a large yawn. He has only a few hours to recuperate before his turn at guard duty.

Encouraged by the friendly smile from the woman across from her, Marie continues.

But whom is she really addressing now?

"Tell me, this war, was it really so terrible? Was it a real war? It's because my grandfather . . . no one really talks about it . . . I don't even know if he was in it . . . no, I don't think so . . . we would have . . . He prefers to tell us about how it was before. Before the events, as he puts it."

The man does not answer right away. He seems engrossed in a painful reflection.

That was his war. Yes, it was a real war. His father, too, had had his war. And he had gone to it singing "The Marseillaise." Like him. And before him, his father's father, and thus numerous generations caught in the often tragic snares of history. Yes, he had turned twenty, and he had experienced war for himself, too . . . a real war, too . . . yes . . . as appalling as the preceding ones. All wars are terrible in the eyes of those who make them, of those who have to make them—in the name of God, of civilization, of the homeland, of liberty, of revolution . . . Only the epithets change: war of religion, Great War, war of liberation, war of occupation, civil war . . . and whatever side you're on, you have to convince yourself that it is the good side, the good cause, and that violence, acts of violence are at times necessary . . . Don't ask too many questions . . . Battlefields are always riddled with heroes . . . Go to death while singing, while holding up, proudly, the beautiful flag . . . otherwise . . . Dirty war! But has there ever been a clean war, other than in the language of those who, in the comfort of parlors, meeting rooms, and under the spotlights, never needed to wear camouflage outfits, never held a man at gunpoint?

In war, in all wars, the enemy always has the same face. The face of our own death. And no one can bear to find themselves confronted with their own death. So we have to annihilate the one who is facing us, because he releases our hidden fear, so we recognize ourselves in him—so he recognizes himself in us. And it is this image of ourselves that we want to eradicate. To tell ourselves that evil is no longer evil when we have to prevent the worst . . . And all the rest is just deceit, verbiage, needless suffering.

"It was . . . It was . . . a war . . . like all wars. A lot of hatred, injustice, suffering. There were the ones who . . . gave orders . . . and the ones who . . . executed. That is always the way it happens."

He quiets for a moment and then goes on, in a low voice, as if speaking to himself.

"Useless to ask yourself questions . . . to look to debate orders. It was necessary to serve and obey. Even if . . . and at times . . ."

He does not finish the sentence. He now has his eyes fixed on the ground. He seems to be looking for his words, to advance with caution, as if he were on the edge of an abyss and he had to pay very close attention so as not to lose his balance.

She is there, near him. She is following him. She too advances with caution. She begins again carefully:

"You had ... to believe, to obey and ... to fight ... it's that simple, isn't it?"

"Of course ... well ... no, I don't think so. They asked us only to serve and to obey, but ... to believe ... no. It did not go that far. You weren't there to debate. We were doing our duty, that's all."

"You mean that you didn't believe in it? That you didn't believe in that war? In the utility, in the necessity of that war?"

"No, that's not what I meant. I had never set foot in Algeria before, that's all."

... November 1956. Arrival in the port of Algiers. The Ville d'Alger is docked. The crossing was rough. One by one, they emerge from the hold, getting off the boat their legs still shaky and their stomachs upset. With a faltering step, they join in the square set up for assemblies. In the glare of winter's incomparable light, the detachment lines up on the docks. Present ... arms! The trucks start up, the convoy forms. From the white city perceived from afar as a mirage, there remains for him only the shock of the first images. First of all, these phantoms veiled in white* who glide through the streets hugging the walls; the colorful, noisy crowd, the sirens' long howl ... and then, in the barracks, meeting the officers.

... The words float, burst like bubbles on the surface of his consciousness ... Maintaining order. Pacification. Your mission, our mission: crush the rebellion. By all means! Dismissed!

Then, everything gets confusing. Orchards and rich plains of the Mitidja, sharp rocks cutting into the gorges of Chiffa, going through villages so similar to villages of France, down to the sound of church bells resonating in the evening sweetness,

---

* A reference to *haïks*, white garments some Algerian women wrap around their heads and bodies. — *Trans.*

shaded squares, town halls with the tricolor flag flying over them . . . Algeria is a French department, who could doubt it?

Yet at times, standing still on the roadside, barefoot children, in rags, watch the military trucks pass, and men, most of them old and dressed in their ample earthen colored burnouses, look away as they pass. And then, here and there, perched on peaks, at the end of torturous paths, a few, small, squalid-looking houses tightly assembled; the douars.

. . . And finally . . . first roundups . . . Preceded by armored tanks and jeeps, they advance before the fearful looks of women standing on the doorsteps of their houses, and who, seeing them approach, veil their heads, gather their children around them, in a pathetic reflex to protect . . .

The night is racked by the motors of armored tanks and trucks, which cross the village in uninterrupted processions. Her eyes open, she watches, listens, and falls asleep a very long while after the noise has dissipated. At times, flurries of machine-gun fire or flare shells shot from the mountain right across from the house, and that makes fleeting menacing gleams of light suddenly surge into the room before fading out in a long whistle. She gets up in the dark and goes to join her mother who hugs her very tightly against her. The next day, while going to school with her classmates, she follows the traces of the treads left by the wheels of tanks on the asphalt.

She keeps going forward slowly, cautiously:

"But it's very distant now . . . you must not be able to re-member anymore . . . and then it had to be . . . so . . ."

"No. Everything is still there. But you know . . . we . . . no . . . no one . . . no one ever . . ."

They were not "one." They were a whole. They were all caught up in a tornado . . . The ceaseless impression of falling into a deeper and deeper abyss, without any other possibility except to attempt to hold on to . . . to what? To the necessary and virile fraternity of men in combat. To orders received and to obligatory obedience. To the certainties that end up settling

in and that very quickly sweep away all the other certainties.
So quickly that you do not even have time to look around and
to remember who you were in another life, in another world.

And it is on the strength of these new convictions, very
quickly consumed, that you draw strength, hereafter and espe-
cially the ineffable sentiment of belonging to a community
of courageous men, resolved and ready to confront the eyes of
these men, eyes full of . . . of what? The eyes of these coarse,
unarmed men, taken in a roundup after an attack, and whom in
the guise of a reprisal, we keep on their knees for hours, hands
on their heads, in the sun or in the rain. With, from time to time,
a kick in the ribs to help them straighten up when they flag.
Or a hit with a gun butt so that they lower their head. All, yes,
they are all cutthroats . . .

Her eyes lowered, Marie listens. Nothing has yet been said.
But she feels in the voices of this man and of this woman who
calmly, politely debate, she feels agitation, a stir come from
afar, from very much further back than the words she hears.
She turns her head slowly toward the man who nervously crum-
ples the newspaper he has in his hands.

"But . . . I don't understand . . . I don't understand why no one
wants to talk about it. To talk . . . simply . . . to tell . . . even in
the lycée . . . you'd think that . . . I don't know, for such a . . ."

He interrupts her softly:

"Marie, your name is Marie, right? Forty years have
passed . . . we can't forget, it's true. But . . . we can . . . we can
be silent. We have the right . . . maybe it's our only one . . ."

In almost the same tone, the woman finishes the sentence:

"The only recourse . . . or if you prefer the only remedy . . .
yes . . . yes . . . practiced by everyone, without consulting
each other, without exchanging hints, yes . . . you could put
it that way, practice the culture of silence . . . to protect yourself. Maybe . . . but that doesn't change anything about each
other's suffering; we can simply try to hold it at a distance,
that's all, don't you think? And when the moment comes to . . .
because it ends up sooner or later coming back up to the surface, doesn't it?"

He doesn't answer the question. He slowly shakes his head.

"There are other ways of . . . As for me, I got out. All I can say is . . . it's this war, these few months, which determined my life, which changed the course of it. When I got back, I decided to go back to school; I wanted to be a doctor. I worked for years, day and night. And it wasn't easy. But I held out. As for the rest . . ."

As he talks, Marie eyes him. She picks up on the spasmodic shiver of his right eyelid—a slight contraction that extends bit by bit over the entire right side of his face. She waits. And since he does not finish his sentence, almost timidly, at the end of a long silence, she suggests in a very calm voice:

"I think that's fitting . . . Medicine . . . That's what I'd like to do too. That could be a response . . . well . . . a way of . . . repairing, I mean . . . to make oneself useful . . . perhaps . . . yes . . . a doctor . . . or a teacher."

The man responds with an impressive calm. He expresses himself in perfect French, almost without an accent. Astonishing for an Arab! He is a robust, squat man, with a plump face, with round glasses ringed in black behind which his eyes seem tiny. The very appearance of a family man, tranquil and debonair. Sitting behind the little table that serves as a desk, Jean finishes filling out the form. Then he raises his head and observes him. A dark gray woolen suit, white shirt . . . A little too assertive, he says to himself. Different from the others. From the ones who arrive quaking with fear even before it begins. He could not address him informally, as he quite naturally could with the others. He cannot even explain to himself why. He is a little annoyed with himself for that. The man standing in the middle of the dimly lit room looks around him. They are alone. They have nothing to say to each other. Introductions are over. His colleagues are not down yet. They are busy with the others. A choice cartload, they warned him. That one there, that guy is one of the two teachers. The intellectual of the group.

The lieutenant pokes his head through the door: We are going to keep that one for the end. Give each man his due! That

*way, he may perhaps have the time to think! Then he closes
the door.*

Without picking up on what has just been said, the woman
starts to speak. She turns to the young woman seated across
from her and who is listening to her attentively.

"In our country, there have also been . . . there are still
silences . . . our history is full of blanks,* even the history of
this war. For years, we have heard only one refrain, sung to
the same tune. A patriotic tune, surely. And it continues . . .
Our fathers were all heroes. Well, almost all of them . . . let's
say . . . an overwhelming majority. Yes, overwhelming. By the
weight and the place it still occupies today. And who knew how
to erase all that could stain the glorious revolution. Only the
heroes have the right to talk. Our heroes have all the rights . . .
they can allow themselves to do anything. And they were well
schooled . . . at least the ones who are still alive. And they speak
so loudly that they may think we hear only them. And that cuts
through the silence and the lies of the torturers, and the complicit silence of those who cannot look their history in the face."

*Around the now-seated man, they are three. Captain Fleury
settled himself on the edge of the table. Standing near the door,
a soldier in khakis, fingers in his belt loops, observes the scene
with an indifferent air. Jean holds the sheet out to the silent
man. He has drawn an organigram,† a pyramid composed of
several triangles. Names are logged and boxed in the angle
of each line. Some of the boxes have no label.*

*Hey teacher, you know how to write, don't you! You're
not like the others. Okay fine, you were on strike, but that . . .
We're not asking you to talk. Here, take the pen! Write! You
see? Right there . . . and right there! We know you know the*

---

* *"Blanc"* in French can mean both "blank" and "white," the color of
mourning in Algeria.—*Trans.*
† French officials made these types of flowcharts or organigrams during
the Algerian War for Independence to chart those involved in resistance
cells.—*Trans.*

names! Fill in the blanks. That's all we're asking you. That way, no one can say that you talked. Tomorrow morning you will be reunited with your children, you can hold your wife in your arms. Your wife, what's her name? You don't want to say it? That's true, Arabs, they don't like talking about their wives. That doesn't mean that they don't love them any less than we others do, huh? A little woman in a bed is good and warm . . . at this hour, she has to be crying her eyes out, poor thing . . . and your children? Aren't you thinking about your children? No, of course not . . . you didn't think about them before, I don't see why you would think about them now . . . and this one wants to make a revolution.

Jean attempts to catch the eye of the man who keeps his head obstinately lowered. The captain straightens up. He lights a Bastos that he holds out to the man. Here, how about a smoke? Oh, excuse me! The gentleman does not smoke. The fellagas *don't allow it, it's true, I had forgotten! They don't smoke, they don't drink . . . I'm telling you . . . all saints! Haven't ya seen men with cut noses and split lips? That's what they do to them, your friends, isn't it? And it's not a pretty sight . . . So! Listen to what I'm proposing to you. We're all going to go next door and we'll leave you alone. You'll have the time to think it over calmly . . .*

As he rises, a terrible howl coming from a neighboring room makes them all shudder. With an air of annoyance, the captain shrugs his shoulders. Before going out, he looks back at Jean who has gotten up to follow him. You, you're staying here, I'm going to see what's happening . . . The man finally raises his head and looks at Jean, right in the eyes.

The trip continues. Interrupted by stops that they do not even seem to notice anymore. Silence has now crept in. The woman has picked up her book again. She continues reading, without retaining or understanding a single one of the sentences that she nevertheless tries hard to reread several times. The young woman curls up wedged in a corner. Her eyes are closed, but she is not sleeping. From time to time, she half-opens her eyes and looks at her two neighbors. The man has not picked up his newspaper again. He stares fixedly at the darkness beyond the window, perhaps attempting to capture a few glimmers of light. The woman observes the man's reflection in the glass. The dark circles have become deeper, and his eyes now seem more sunken. The wrinkles at the corners of his lips are more marked and his emerging beard shadows his face in places with bluish stains. He looks so tired!

"I was observing him with his gray hair and always badly shaven beard, his deeply furrowed brows, his wrinkles running from the sides of his nose to the corners of his mouth. I was waiting."

She waits, without impatience. They have not yet arrived at their destination. She knows it. She doesn't need to look at her watch.

She suddenly feels far away . . . far away from all that.

She is sitting on the edge of a pond. Leaning over the water, she observes the froth that once in a while comes to trouble the stagnant surface. Bubbles burst all over, dissolve in concentric waves and almost at once the water closes in on itself again, for an instant. Under the thin greenish film, she guesses its depth, the underground life, the secret swarming, the palpitations that skim the surface with a slight stir very quickly erased, and in no way disturb the apparent calm that reigns in this place.

He finally decides to turn his head. He seems infinitely weary.

"Your father was a schoolteacher in Boghari, is that it?"

"Yes."

"And he . . . he died . . ."

"During the war."

"Ah!"

He remains silent a few seconds before adding:

"I didn't stay over there for long."

"But you remember what you saw in the camp, don't you? The few months you spent back there, you remember them pretty well, I believe . . . That's what you said. You were there in February? February 1957. During the strike imposed by the FLN . . ."

" . . . "

"Maybe you even met him . . . You might have . . ."

"Who? Your father?"

"He was kidnapped with his brother, his cousin, and still others . . . Eight men in all . . . taken out of their homes in the dead of night, by soldiers."

"Many men were taken to the camps . . . every day . . ."

"We never saw them again. Maybe . . . but no, that would be too much . . ."

"You know . . . there were so many arrests the whole time I was there. I know that . . . I was in charge of registering the ones who came in."

"That's it? So you never saw anything, ever? Never heard anything? Tallying up the entries and watching those who kept up enough strength to try to run away after the torture sessions, that was your job, nothing but that, right? And yes . . . among the ones who were arrested there were not many who got out again, or well . . ."

"The ones who were brought to us were suspects. We had to take the time to . . . to interrogate them . . . for the purposes of the investigation."

"Of course, they had to be made to talk. But that had nothing to do with you, of course . . ."

"No one got out of this war unscathed! No one! You hear!"

The exclamation resounds like the noise of a door being slammed. He abruptly raised his voice, as if he wanted to convince her, to silence her maybe. But is this the only object of his anger?

Marie sat up straight. She gets up abruptly and goes to sit next to the woman. She softly tells the man, who is now facing her:

"And the ones who refused to talk . . . to say what they knew. Is it true that they were tortured?"

"There were special sections in the intelligence service. It was war . . ."

He takes his head in his hands, in the same gesture as the woman a few instants before. All that they can see is the top of his head, slightly balding, shoulders sagging.

*Go on! And above all, don't let yourselves be had if they
claim not to know anything. They all end up talking . . . They
give names, most often, just any old one. The shitty thing is, we
can't even take the time to check. Not right away. First of all
the job has to be done. Some are tougher than others. And then,
we have to pull out the big guns. Mustn't hesitate!*

He again raises his head:
"Yes. Some. We couldn't do otherwise. But only if they refused to collaborate. It was necessary to . . ."
He stops himself just before saying . . . he was going to say . . .
"to crush the rebellion." Thus, the words are still imprinted in
his memory. After so many years, he effortlessly retrieved the
same words, the same arguments: refusal to collaborate, rebellion, pacification, interrogations, prioritized investigations for
intelligence, prevention, protection of European civilians . . . so
nothing is erased. But *that* word . . . never! People never spoke
about torture, about brutality . . . no. These interrogations
were . . . harsh, some would even say . . . vigorous. To obtain
the maximum information. That was the consecrated formula.
Interrogations pushed sometimes until . . .
Marie looks at the woman.
"Your father was . . ."
"He was tortured. With his companions. For a night. An
entire night. And then executed . . . with several bullets. That's
what they told us. 'Shot down while he was trying to run.' Official version. Retold by the newspapers from that time. That's
what they called 'firewood duty.' That's how they used to get
rid of . . ."
She turns to look at the man and stares at him fixedly,
straight in the eyes. She gestures toward the young woman:
"You have to know what it is, right? Explain to her what
'firewood duty' was, explain it to her, tell her since she knows
nothing about this war, since her grandfather has told her nothing more than about his thrilling fishing excursions in Algeria."
Even before he reacts, she begins like a person telling a story:
"There was wood in the forest of Mongorno . . . a few kilometers from Boghari, not very far from the forest of Boghar . . .

beautiful timber . . . and as winters were very cold, you had to get warm in the barracks and in the camps. The problem is that all the prisoners who were sent to look for wood would never come back. You know why? Do tell, you who remember the winters over there. Unless . . ."

The jeep just started. At the steering wheel, Claude hesitates a few seconds about which path to take. It doesn't make much difference, all of the zone is secured. He starts down the first path on the right and curses about the numerous ruts that shake the vehicle and slow his advance. Above him, the trees' foliage merges and forms a canopy pierced with beams of light. It could've been a swell jaunt! He turns to look at his silent companion. Too taciturn, Jean! He barely lets a sound escape his lips. For the last few days, he has changed . . . he cuts himself off . . . You'd say he was doing too much thinking. Should keep an eye on him! Until we send him for disciplinary actions . . .

He comes out into a clearing, stops and turns off the ignition. One hand on the steering wheel, he turns to look at Jean. Your turn now! Getting out?

In less than a quarter of an hour, it is all over. Jean has unloaded the eight bodies that now lie on the ground. Claude gives him a friendly punch on the shoulder. Don't worry about it, old chap, we will find them tomorrow! Eight fellagas *taken prisoner, shot down in the forest while they were attempting to run during firewood duty. Nice catch, right? You can even add that they did not respond to the summons . . . if that does you good . . . Jean gets back in the jeep and settles on the seat next to him without responding.*

The rest of the sentence gets lost in the abrupt intake of air at the tunnel's entrance, which makes them all jump. The train slows. The compartment appears suddenly brighter. In the neon lights, the man's face is ashen. The woman is now hunched over.

Marie remained silent. Then she abruptly sits up straight. She lays her hand on the arm of the woman, who shrinks at this contact.

"He doesn't understand. He doesn't understand you. Look, he cannot even speak anymore . . ."

The woman murmurs:

"Like all the others. First blind and deaf, and for a long time . . . mute . . . and who even suffer from amnesia . . ."

Now, she is quiet. Even if all has not been said, even if a painful palpitation still makes her shiver, something has come unknotted in her. Whether it is he or someone else, it does not matter. She tells herself that nothing resembles her childhood dreams, that executioners have a man's face, she is sure of it now, they have a man's hands, at times even a man's reactions and nothing allows them to be distinguished from others. And this idea terrifies her a bit more.

Marie begins again:

"I think we will be there soon."

Travelers with loaded luggage pass in the corridor while debating in loud voices.

"Next stop . . . last stop! The train is coming into the station."

As if to rouse herself, Marie shakes her head, making her hair swirl in a movement full of grace, before fastening it with a barrette, which she pulls out of the pocket of her jeans.

She rises, goes to open the door, takes a few steps in the corridor.

Face to face, the man and the woman do not move.

She expects nothing. She knows there is nothing to expect. She looks at him, she observes him, she analyzes him, attentively, minutely, as if she wanted to fix each feature of this face in her memory. He has lowered eyes, hands placed on his knees. He is not trying to steal away. She closes her book again, and puts it back in her bag. She counted on finishing it during the trip, but she has not progressed very much in the discovery of this story that issued from another war. It doesn't make much difference. She has time to read, to look for answers. A lot of time . . . maybe she will be somewhere else. Maybe it will be another day. She will make other trips.

She gets up to slip on her coat. She says loudly, as if she were alone in the compartment:

"Too bad . . . it's dark out. We can't see the sea."

Marie comes back. She takes her backpack, smiles at the woman, and points to the suitcase.

"May I help you?"

"No, no, thanks . . . it's not that heavy . . ."

The man has already grabbed the suitcase.

"May I?"

She doesn't answer.

On the doorstep, Marie waves her hand and goes away with a light step.

In her turn, she picks up her handbag and makes for the exit. Carrying the suitcase and the tote bag, he follows her. She goes down the steps and stops on the platform. She looks back. He is behind her and holds the suitcase out to her.

Before she even has time to open her mouth to thank him, he says:

"I wanted to tell you . . . it seems to me . . . yes . . . you have the same eyes as . . . the same look as . . . as your father. You look a lot like him."

APPENDIX

Nationality Certificate

The administrator of the mixed community of Boghari, undersigned, certifies that the individual named Benameur Yagoub, Mohammed, Yagoub, born on November 10, 1919 [place illegible], is of French nationality. (Muslim native Algerian not naturalized French). To attest good faith the present certificate has been issued to attest to his rights.

Boghari, the twenty-third of December,
nineteen hundred and forty.
For the head administrator
The vice-minister
B. de [name illegible]
[Commune Mixte de Boghari, Dept d'Alger]

CE 55310

Certificat de Nationalité.

L'Administrateur de la Commune mixte de
Boghari, soussigné, certifie que le Nommé
Benamer Yagoub ? Mohammed ? Yagoub
né le 10 Novembre 1919 au Douar Beni St Féli?
est de Nationalité française (Indigène Musulman
Algerien non naturalisé français).

En foi de quoi le présent certificat
a été délivré pour valoir ce que de droit.

Boghari le vingt trois décembre milneufcent quarante
Pour l'Administrateur ppal
L'adjoint

Certificate of Good Social and Moral Standing

Mixed community of Boghari

We, administrator of the mixed community of Boghari, certify that the named Benameur Yagoub [name illegible] Mohammed, pursuing a career as Schoolteacher residing at [place illegible] is of good social and moral standing and his conduct has always been proper and irreproachable during his stay in the mixed community of Boghari.

In good faith of which we have accorded him the present certificate to justify fair request.

In Boghari, December 10, 1940.
For the Head Administrator,
The vice-administrator
Algiers, 25 Sept. 1946

CERTIFICAT
de Bonnes Vie et Mœurs

COMMUNE _Mixte de Boghari_

Nous, _Administrateur de la Commune mixte de Boghari_ , certifions que l _e nommé Benamer Yagoub & Hadj Mohammed_

exerçant la profession de _Instituteur_

demeurant à _Ouled Antar_

est de bonnes vie et mœurs et que sa conduite a toujours été

régulière et irréprochable _durant son séjour dans l'_

Commune mixte de Boghari

En foi de quoi nous lui avons accordé le présent certificat

pour lui servir et valoir ce que de raison.

A _Boghari_ le _10 décembre 1934_

P^r l'Administrateur par
l'Adjoint,

Communes n° 532
BLIDA. — IMP. ADM. A. MAUGUIN
3 II-7-36

The Inspector of the Académie d'Alger

To Monsieur Benameur Teacher [word illegible] in Boghari

I have the honor of informing you that, by rectoral decree of 25 Sept. 1946, you were named in the capacity of Teaching Assistant in the school of g. M.M. de Boghari a temporary position replacing M. extended.

Please arrive at your new position on 1 Oct. 1946.

You will be briefed by *M. le* [blank] to whom you will communicate the present notice, which will serve as your nomination.

The minutes relative to your nomination, established on the attached printed sheet, and signed by *M. le chef de la commune,* should be addressed directly to me the day following your arrival, in the absence of which it would be impossible for me to compensate you financially during the desired period. You should, therefore, take care to notify *M. l'Inspecteur primaire* of your district in writing about the date of your official arrival.

For the personnel of Alger-ville, the formalities will be performed by the school's principal or director, who will see to the necessary correction of the attached printed document and append the school's seal.

Alger, le _25 SEPT 1946_ 194

AVIS A CONSERVER

La correspondance doit toujours être établie sur du papier blanc (format 21" X 27")

L'Inspecteur d'Académie d'Alger

à Monsieur Benamar Instit

inst.   à Boghari

J'ai l'honneur de vous informer que, par arrêté
rectoral du _25 SEPT 1946_ vous
avez été _nommé_ en qualité d'Institut*eur-adj*
à _l'école de g. F.7 de Boghari_
à titre provisoire

en remplacement de M. _maintenu_

Je vous prie de vous rendre à votre nouveau poste pour
le _1er oct. 1946_

Vous y serez installé par M. le
à qui vous communiquerez le présent avis qui tient lieu
d'arrêté de nomination.

Le procès-verbal d'installation, établi sur l'imprimé ci-
contre, et signé par M. le Chef de la Commune, devra m'être
adressé **directement** le lendemain de votre arrivée, faute
de quoi, il me serait impossible de vous faire mandater votre
traitement en temps voulu. Vous aurez soin, en outre, de
faire connaître, par lettre, la date de votre installation à
M. l'Inspecteur primaire de votre circonscription.

NOTA. — Pour le personnel d'Alger-ville l'installation sera faite par le
Directeur ou la Directrice de l'école. Prévoir les corrections nécessaires sur
l'imprimé ci-joint et apposer le cachet de l'école.

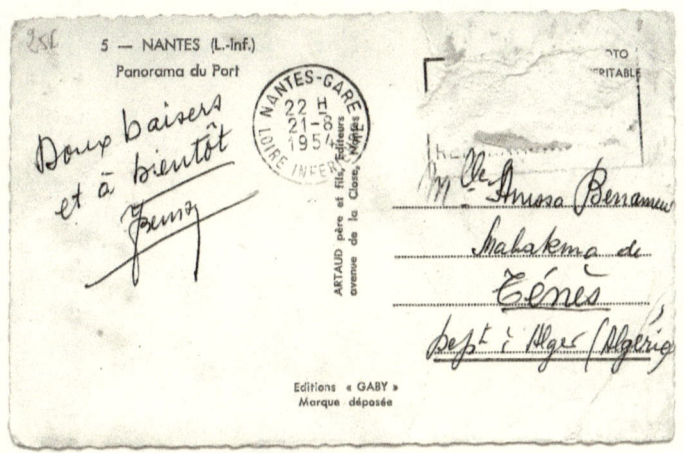

The beautiful handwriting of the schoolteacher.

Loving kisses and see you soon.

Mlle Anissa Benameur
Mabakma de Ténès
Department of Algiers (Algeria)

UNDER
THE JASMINE
AT NIGHT

STORIES

To Christiane, the friend regained

CONTENTS

UNDER THE JASMINE AT NIGHT

Bent over her, he watches her sleep. Lips half-open, soft breathing, eyes shut over visions, dreams that exclude him, he does not doubt it. In the bedroom scarcely lit by the small lamp that he leaves on late into the night, everything is quiet. Bent over her, he looks at this supple body, relaxed on the wrinkled sheets. He just possessed her. Took her. Penetrated her. Apparently. Just took what was given to him. Apparently. Now he spies on this unchecked body, submerged in a space that he cannot attain, that he cannot embrace. Bent over her, he seeks to cross the borders of these forbidden places. She is elsewhere, alone. Alone? If he could only be sure. How to grasp this part of her that eludes him? Bent over her, he scrutinizes her face. Attentively. This quiver at the corners of her mouth, isn't it the trace of a smile, the abrupt way she blinks her eyes, the slow sigh coming from deep within her that runs over her body in a barely perceptible undulation, isn't it . . . She shakes her shoulders slightly, as if to get rid of a burden, turns her head away, lays her cheek on her hand, conceals her face from him and continues to dream. Then she lifts her arm and grips the sheet in her hand, biting her lips abruptly. In a movement of rage, he straightens, clenches his fists as the desire to call her rises within him, to shake her viciously to make her regain consciousness, to let her know that he is there. That she cannot go away without him. The sleeping woman's breathing becomes more rapid. Fluttering eyelashes, hasty breaths, suddenly her body stiffens, contorts, and little by little relaxes, surrenders. Toward what lonely voyage is she being swept without his being able to hold her back, to bring her back to him, or even to follow her? Her bare shoulder shines in the half light, round, golden, textured skin. He raises his hand as if in a caress, but lets it fall again, needlessly. How to be sure that behind her shut eyes

Very quickly, faced with this look fixed on her, she pretended to sleep. She controls her breathing, slowing its rhythm, slow breath, then regular, eyes sealed shut, entire body relaxes, progressive relaxation, until the feigned surrender of sleep. He didn't turn out the light. Not yet. Every night he wants to see her body, her eyes, her face until the irresistible surge of pleasure. As for her, she shuts her eyes in the swell, and lets him revel in her body [given, taken, worked over]. He will turn off the light only very far into the night. She lets herself slowly slip into a half consciousness on happy shores and drifts without landmarks in a slightly bluish foggy universe, crisscrossed from time to time with flashes of light. She runs on the side of a dusty path, a powdery trail bordered by high dark mountains, she runs barefoot, in the sun, entirely tense with the desire to arrive there, to the edge of the river whose haunting babble she hears. Airily, she runs covered with a veil of red dust, with a halo of light that envelops her, protects her. Her feet leave no trace on the path and she advances, guided by the certainty that one day she will have to scale the mountains, thwart the obstacles if she wants to arrive there. Gazes follow her, thousands of avid gazes, irradiant, shards of obsidian suspended in the sky, she feels the bite on her body, on her bare legs on her face whipped by tremendous winds, on her bare shoulders, but she continues, she runs, she goes farther away. Still faster, still farther.

Morning movements. Opening his eyes, guessing by the brightness that bathes the bedroom that it's almost time to get up and to leave. He stretches out his arm. Next to him, her place is empty but still warm. She rose noiselessly so as not to disturb his slumber. Morning sounds. Dishes softly clinking, smell of coffee. He shuts his eyes again. As soon as she has prepared everything, she will come into the bedroom and open the blinds. That's how she wakes him, by chasing away the night. Without saying a word. Without pronouncing his name. She busies herself in the kitchen. She walks barefoot, he does not hear her come in. He never hears her. Barely even a slight footfall. And then eventually the very near rustle of her dress as she heads toward the window. Need to stretch, his eyes half-closed to contemplate her body her breasts stiff under the silken fabric. Morning vision. Mouth shut over the words that he doesn't know how to say. Only clearing his throat. Eyes half-closed, he watches her, his body still heavy just this thought erupting in the depths of his silence she is mine. In the day that is beginning, this

She hums. Barely a murmur. Indistinct words. There are always words of love in the songs that come to her lips. She lets the water run for a long time. So that it is cool enough to bring her back to life each morning. Then to spray her arms, her face to collect dewy drops source of crystal song to leap on cliffs while listening to the rustle of the leaves rocked by a sea breeze. *Oh my garden of cool water and shadow** the windows are open and the sun without waiting has slipped into the heart of a smile come to her lips, she does not know how she does not know why. It will be a beautiful day. Barefoot on the white, cool tile, she busies herself in the kitchen. On the table, the cup of nice warm milk the steaming coffeepot the ashtray with streaks of mother of pearl to look at the steam playing in wisps in the view skewed through a slanted ray of sunlight as he drinks his coffee. Behind the door, children rush down the stairs, call to each other, greet each other with loud shouts and go out. Morning noises, days' cadence. Mysterious and soft song, refrain that will follow her all day long. To retrieve the words of this air that sings within her *under the jasmine at night*† yes that song from bygone days has come to her lips she does not know how she does not know why *under*

---

*From a 1963 poem by Louis Aragon, *"Hereux celui qui meurt d'aimer"* ("Happy is the man who dies of love"), set to music and sung by Jean Ferrat in 1971.—*Trans.*

† *"Taht el Yasmina fellil"* (*"Sous le jasmin la nuit"*/"Under the jasmine at night") is a revolutionary Tunisian song of love and war.—*Trans.*

the jasmine at night maybe that's it, only the smell, not the darkness.

Before closing the door again, he calls to her. Maya. He repeats her name without quite knowing why. Maya. She appears on the threshold of the bedroom, her head haloed with light. She is waiting. Standing in the door frame he does not see the features of her face. He doesn't know if she is looking at him, if she is smiling at him, attentive to only what he can grasp of her and take away with him. Halo of light transparency of the day. She comes closer, ready to listen, to obey. Certainly. He turns his face away. He goes out. He walks slowly. Behind him the door closes again. Softly. He descends the steps. The street is already flooded with sun. Up above, the windows are open. It would be enough for him to look back, maybe that way he could

Immobile near the door, her upright body graceful and still young soft, she hears within her the echo of his voice. Her name. Maya. She sings. Louder now. Why wouldn't she sing? Her name hers softly andante violins in cascades at the heart of the day begun again. Something within her a subtle shiver tender solitude *"a shiver of water on moss."** To put into words what grows impatient within her, this incredible slowness which gives her languid gestures now that she is alone. Going through the day conducive to expectations, to dreams mirages presently crowding in. She has in her hands only a fragile sliver of moon stolen from the night. Does not want to break what could only be an illusion. Baby steps, she goes, she runs through the morning alone, she sometimes hesitates in front of the door she closed herself then turns away, continues on her way.

All day he thinks of what he cannot grasp of her. This mysterious smile on her lips in the heart of sleep. Her eyes lowered

---

* From the Léo Ferré song *"Écoutez la chanson bien douce"* ("Listen to this very sweet song"), from the 1878 Paul Verlaine poem of the same title. —*Trans.*

to avoid looking at him. Troubled, deep waters. What does she have buried deep inside her? How does one get through this slight stiffness which tightens her muscles when he places his hands on . . . How to possess her entirely, fully, to fill her with himself, with *his* smell, with his breath, with his image, with his name? How to chain her, to constrain her, to reduce her, to erase the dreams which sweep her away from him? Yes, he repeats to himself annoyed, irritated, tormented, to reduce her, so that she belongs only to me, potions and spells, to go all the way to break the shell, to extract from her everything that makes her so remote, inaccessible, as if

A full life. Why does she have a sharp pang in the back of her throat like a scruple? A distress which overflows, spreads and grows day after day. Days too often surrounded with gray. She does not know what creates the strange disconcerting turmoil that from time to time rumbles within her. She is not unhappy oh no this word does not suit her. No. But she does not know how to put into words what she lacks either shriveling stalemate. Still even more. Like a plant which perishes even as she has everything needed to bloom, water light earth air refreshed as regularly as possible. What more could she desire and why does she feel so dry, arid, impenetrable, unfeeling, as if the water washing over her folded wings without being able to reach her roots and was poured all around. Needlessly. When the winds come off the shoreline shake the trees' branches, the most fragile leaves come off and fall to the ground and rot. Slowly. Maybe that's what it is. Slow, irremediable rot, one by one the illusions come off, fall on the ground—slow whirlwinds—are crushed by men's steps, are corrupted rot. Irremediably. How does one make sure not to

He walks. The entire weight of the sun on his back. The sun has a sex in our country, it's feminine. The night too. He stops as if gripped by this obvious fact. Around him, men come and go calmly hemmed in by secular certainties. Penetrated with their strength, with their truth. Man power. Never questioned. Illusions. He walks. They recognize him. They greet him. They move out of the way. He is at home everywhere. No one can get in his way.

Only her.

Consuming worry. To crush her, with the mere strength of his certainties. With his virile will. When he thinks about her, he feels caught up, irresistibly attracted toward a chasm full of hostile, moving shadows. Swept away by punches by kicks by bouts of anger all of which stand between her and him. To face the shadows. What more could she desire? She has everything she needs to be happy. But this malaise. But this fleeting look. This excessive submissiveness. These masks which she never removes.

Around him, men unhurriedly come and go. That's it. They are at home everywhere. Do they only know

Colors of the day bathed in expectation. Every day on the balcony she enumerates the shades. Blue sky bathed in waiting. Indefinitely. And her child running toward her, finally awake. She takes him in her arms, hugs him, breathes in his smell, so nice and sweet, soaks it in before he grows up, before he escapes her, before he becomes a man. He puts his hands around her neck he snuggles even closer to her. There, right against her, fragile, vulnerable, anything could harm him. She shivers. She imagines his voice later on. His manly voice. His manly hands. Hands resting on a woman's body. To caress. Perhaps. Perhaps he will know *"how to fill a trembling body with stars."* He murmurs a few words into her ear. Loving words. She is sure, even if she does not understand. Murmured words always have meaning, even if she does not understand. The ones who impart them know. The ones on the receiving end know. Only them. Up above, silver disk shot through with shadows on the blue sky, the moon has decidedly forgotten to retire. The moon in bright sunshine, what indecency. She smiles. Memories of the playground. Smells of paths lined with rosemary, quivering with girls' secrets. She wraps jasmine chains around her wrists, she bends over.

---

* From the 1968 Jacques Brel song *"J'arrive"* ("I'm coming"). —*Trans.*

A little way farther down, in the street, men unhurriedly
come and go, an incessant flow whose babble comes to her.
Just a far-off babble.

He is alone in his office. He knows at this moment she carries
her child in her arms and that bent over him she speaks motherly words to him. Strange words that he does not understand.
Probably because no one ever . . . Her son. He does not know
how to say *our* child, the child is still so very much hers. He
remembers the slow mystery that grew within her, her body
inhabited, [absent, closed-off, attentive] that worried wait, her
far-off look, still farther off. His insatiable desire for her still.
Of what she concealed. A handsome child. A boy who will be
a man. Who will escape her. Who will go away from her. Irremediably. Who will make her suffer. Perhaps. He stands up
straight. Opens his files. Turns pages. With a flick of his pen
underlines, crosses out, scrawls. With a call, doors open, and
standing before him, men bow their heads, spill out their pleas,
quiet when he gives them the order to. Servile, docile, trembling. With an impatient gesture he pushes aside the grievances
and they retire in silence. Court is adjourned. Power. Might.
He can. He just has to will it. He promises himself that one day

She rises. In the kitchen, she stands still for an instant. He is
going to be home soon. The day ends. Darkness comes. The air
is cooler on the hillsides, the cornflowers are blooming splashes
poppy's blood needless wounds. She closes the windows. The
child is asleep now. The two of them walked for a long time
in the city's streets. The good respectable mother and child.
Her nose on the cold pane [hard smooth icy] she stares fixedly
at the flickering points of light soon snuffed out weakened by
the steam. Hand in hand, they walked a long time in the city's
streets. Playing at drowning themselves in the wave, waves in
timid onslaughts at first, licking her feet in slow caresses then
rising, unfurling tides and even more, this man's gaze on her
[insistent precise brutal] that's it desirous violating she fled,
took her child in her arms, fragile rampart, vulnerable no nothing should steer her off her path.

This exasperation that rises within him. That travels upward. Opens chinks then moves in, clings. Gnaws at him little by little. His gestures become violent. His voice imperious. He no longer looks at her. So he decided. To make her fold. To put out the creeping fire that devours her. That consumes her. That consumes him. So that she finally knows. May the demons finally escape from their dark cavern. May fear finally be read in her gaze, in her movements [tamed submitted vanquished] day after day. May night swallow her dreams again become a private domain that he can labor in as he sees fit.

Blind, lost, she advances in a maze of streets, badly bruised, hands bloody with the number of times that they've hit against the walls that hem her in. Hold herself back so as not to fall. She skirts immense stakes traverses seasons she advances does not look back guided by the colors that block out her horizon. Red is fantastic. It twists under her feet and its incandescence goes through her flesh, necessary wound so that she can orientate herself. Blue is fierce, it vibrates like a scream before letting itself die vanquished by the shadows. Green immobile sentinel on the threshold of open grottos on the burned earth. That is when she presses on into the immensity of white with the transparency of puddles left by the storm as her only landmarks. She splashes she stumbles falls gets up holds onto the underbrush covered in snow she trembles she calls she only hears the echo of this slow howl that comes out of her and shatters against our silences.

Bent over her, he looks at her. She seems to be in a deep sleep. Totally submerged. He hears her haphazard heartbeat. Suddenly, this certainty that it would be enough for him to hold his hand out to her so that she comes to the surface. He knows that in this instant. Her bare shoulder shines in the semi-darkness. He raises his arm as if to open her eyes, surprises his movement, his hand raised [hesitant stretched out undecided] his trembling hand. Hanging over her. She does not close her eyes again. Does not turn her head away. She simply looks at him.

ON THIS LAST MORNING

She finally lets herself fall back on her bed, in the final exhaustion, all her mental faculties focused on the desire to keep her perceptions intact, an acute desire that she decodes without surprise, a desire to make this final presence among others last.

Gone, the spreading pain that in little scattered clusters had totally taken possession of her body, disintegrating up to the consciousness that she still belongs to the world of the living.

She is alone facing death. No one is there in this instant when, vanquished, she surrenders without fright to this strange slippage. Neither life, nor wakefulness, nor slumber. A point suspended from which she drifts in a universe that she senses is intermediary, in the unbelievable weightlessness of an instant that she knows to be fragile. Certainties whirl, come closer together then move further away. Loads of questions, more annoying than flies, brush her inert body, linger over her closed or open eyes—she does not know, how could she know?—then they again move to a higher altitude still without disappearing. She must expel all the ones that she will not have time to elucidate. Time? Time lurks above her, still, like a stopped heartbeat whose far-off echoes come strike against the still perceptive edges of her consciousness.

But now she starts to shake with an intense jubilation. The exquisite sensation comes up in waves of an initially blinding brightness. Then she becomes accustomed to it. She explores the shimmers of light more vivid than fireflies, until discovering a wriggling shape. An obvious thing that perches on the corner of her right eyelid. There, now, she knows why. It is because she will be the center of attention. For a few hours, she will be at the center of this day of glory. A little bit like flypaper which will trap the thoughts of the beings that live around her, who are still living, who breathe, and who for the first time—she thinks, in a brief flash, with an irony totally divorced from bitterness "for the first time in my life"—cannot slink away, because that is how it shall be, they have to in their turn accomplish their final obligation to her, to their mother, to their sister, to their grandmother, now dead, now present, all of the obligations which they cannot shirk, all of the ceremonies that accompany death, you have to follow protocol, it's an absolute priority for those who remain. Especially in a family like theirs.

Rachid bends over his mother's body. He can't bear to tell himself that she is now nothing more than this inert form. No, he doesn't want to think of the word corpse. An inert form, still warm, he is sure. He steps back slightly. He continues to scrutinize his mother's face, as he has never done before. At this instant he realizes that he never really looked at her. He used to come see her every day, of course, but he never looked at her. Is it because her eyes are closed that her face seems totally foreign? Her eyes continually alert, but veiled by a too often perceptible distress. An eternal stiffness at the corners of her lips, the still more marked prominence of her nose, her wrinkles, her deeply furrowed brow, everything is still there, but what has changed? Would this already be the death mask? Is this the only imprint that life has left on this still warm body?

He turns his head away, goes toward the window and opens it, as if to expel the hard feelings that are exhaled in the sweltering bedroom. Today he doesn't want to ask himself the questions that have not ceased tormenting him for so many years. Was she happy? He had been looking for the trace of a smile on her face for too long, the gentle touch of happiness. Had she been happy?

He lowers his head, covers his face with his hands. He knows the answer.

Leave her, they tell him, let her go in peace.

Peace. Did she even know what that word meant? And for her, what does peace here and now look like?

She turned twenty. She does not remember. Only the child's cries resound in her memory, her firstborn son, who came very quickly. Too quickly? But . . . how important is that? What else could she expect?

It's in this same bed that the young woman who just gave birth, mask of contentment carefully adjusted on her face, received the homage of those who came to visit her each time she gave birth to a little bitty man. Seven days of glory. Seven sons and three daughters. All living, all handsome, in their father's image. Her pride. Her strength to face life. And later, to take her revenge. Children to act as a counterbalance. To counterbalance the emptiness, the falling out of love then the hatred. To fill a life with whining, tottering, harassing convictions. To fill her role. To empty herself, to fill herself again. Body never desired only taken.

And the glory of each time she became a mother: her stomach which swells, stretches out, quivers and pulsates as if under the influence of an underground swell, that spreads itself out, with at its center the bloom of a mauve flower, hardened breasts, finally heavy, finally rounded, that softly widen, soft prominences, alabaster run through with transparent streaks of blue marble, the brown rings wide around her nipples, pricked with little white grains, and later, after the quickly forgotten pains of childbirth, the ethereal sensation, the shivers of pleasure, which run through her whole body when the little half-open mouth greedily grabs onto her stiffened nipple to extract the sap, which flows from it indefinitely, fullness, the little one who falls asleep, well-fed, very close to her, this heat from a minuscule body, these closed eyes, this face appeased by the happiness of a love which is born at the root of her being, a total love, this close dependency, she is the source, she is the mother, she is the one who has the power to give life, glorious and sovereign in this instant.

And then, at thirty, maybe even before, to avoid completely undressing herself so as not to have to look at, to face the disheartening sight of her stomach, so creased and wrinkled, depressions of flabby flesh under her fingers. And of her breasts prematurely withered, like empty husks.

He is the first one, the beloved, the eldest one, Rachid, he is the one who, bent over her in this instant, gauges the depths of her estrangement. Who is tormented in this instant by waves of regret that he confuses with grief.

Yes you can be proud of your sons. In the eyes of all, they have succeeded in life. What is happiness if not the appearance of stability reinforced by material comfort and the certainty of inspiring respect?

Intolerable lucidity, that still sharpens her consciousness, more intolerable than this fiery blade that when she was living—but had she ever been living?—went through her chest with each of her movements.

Why, in this immobile instant, why before closed eyes is a silhouette being drawn, one that she recognizes immediately, one that she would recognize among all the others, the one of this man so loved, so hated, this stranger who had been her husband, why does she let herself be invaded by the resurgence of another pain, the pain of waiting, the memory of innumerable nights spent waiting for him?

When evenings were exhausted in perfectly tidy motions, immutable rituals, repeated motions, well-oiled mechanism in the tumult of unruly thoughts, when the silence's opaqueness at last moved in with the night, began the wait for the man who never came, who would not come. The man that she knew to be in another woman's arms. Hard, precise images that forced themselves on her, gave rise to a strange febrility that she did not chase away. The wait in solitude was becoming slow agony renewed each night. A waiting period spent alone accompanied by the perceptible breath of others, who were sleeping next door, very near, in the neighboring bedrooms. Yes, the others were sleeping. The others very naturally went into the night, toward the reassurance of sleep. She, seated on a chair, near the door, across from the impeccably tidy bed, because she did not want to unmake it, because she did not want to sleep, because she did not want to forget, she sharpened her suffering to feel herself exist in the shadows that were slowly descending and spreading around the world, erasing every perception other than one of a frightening distress. Biting her knuckles, in silence, clenched fists. Sometimes until she bled. Second after second, on the alert for the too infrequent noise of steps in the street, the too infrequent echoes of voices beyond the closed windows, the creaking of a door that someone has not yet opened, not yet, that no one will open. God's name pronounced a thousand times in vain, without being able to appease the burning in the pit of her stomach, and that rose again, as bitter sap, bitter burning in her throat. Staying there, seated on a chair, still, up straight, until the sky grew paler.

And when, vanquished by the day's transparency, the shadows at last dissipated, the wait was coming to an end.

There, in the brightness that was beginning, slowly, too slowly, standing across from the cold bed, empty, always impeccably tidy, she listened without moving to the call to prayer, then the noises of water, the father's morning ablutions in the neighboring room, then the laughter and voices of the children, who wake up one after the other. Only then did she open the door.

Every night, she turned in circles in the cage of pain.

She turned fifteen . . . but had she ever been a child? From childhood did she ever have the freshness, the candor, the spontaneity? Had she ever known the foolishness of adolescence, the secret hopes, the jitters, the delicate blushes, the impulses?

She had not, she will never have known the upheaval of a first love. The sweetness of a caress, and the burning of a gaze on her desired body. The fever, the irrepressible trembling in the wait for pleasure.

She never knew how to, she never could surrender herself fully. Always on the edge of something. Always held back,

always bound by strings too tight for her to allow herself to kick
up her heels in the least, the least divergence. To dissimulate, to
restrain, to repress, to stifle, forever.

Yes, it is as if she had been dead for a long time. For . . .
for . . . but why is that important? Dead, she already had
been for . . . for . . . since she did not exist in that absent man's
eyes, always absent, even when he was near her.

And yet, there it comes back, like a suggestive point of sweetness or pain, the retrieved memory of the man's hands, the only
man who had ever touched her, her children's father. She starts
to look obstinately for the memory of the contact of his hands.
It seems to her that something come from very far, very deep
within her, starts to shake, to quiver. An insane hope begins
hammering at her temples. She wants to, she wants to hold it
back. In vain. In this instant she only retrieves the sensation
of having been a troublesome presence to him. Of never having existed in his thoughts, in his gaze, under the palms of his
hands, in the hollow of his body.

A body taken, only taken once in a while. Never, no never
ever desired.

Only the gaze of another burst forth.

That man. A worker that came each day to work on the
plumbing or the masonry in the house being built, just across
from theirs. That gaze that she caught one day when she was
hanging out the laundry on the terrace, her head and her
arms bare, her wet dress stuck to her body.

A window open on the bedroom's emptiness, just across
from the house.

A street to cross.

A door to nudge in the silent deserted afternoons.

A somber, sharp gaze, loaded with desire, that, in the following days, lingered over the half-open window, over the shape of
the shutters, where you could certainly guess a noise, a breath,
a shiver, a chest that was rising, a thrill.

And suddenly, slight rustles cross the space and emanate
around her. A gentle flutter, and then still another. Words, yes,

these are words that flit in dense swarms above her. They skim over her body, she does not really feel the contact but she follows the path, until they form a chain and settle at the spot where the lamentations of memories are all listened to. And these few words that she attempted to bury in the depths of her consciousness for a very long time, fill her ears with a violent disruption: "A door, nothing more than a door to nudge . . ."

IN GOOD FAITH UPON MY HONOR

He told me, from now on you have to learn to live with it.

The IT slammed, like a slap, then started to immeasurably swell, invading the whole room. A latex balloon stretched to the max, ready to explode.

These are his words. Words that gave an unbearable reality to what I already knew and what I didn't want to hear. Because, it's well known, despite what people see, despite what people tell you, we remain persuaded that these things only happen to other people. I kept myself on the outer limits of incredulity, thinking it would be enough for me not to go forward to alter fate. I naively or impudently gulped down certainties sustained by an absurd pride. Not me! Not us! I couldn't lift up my head to look at him again. I knew that he had his eyes fixed on me to better gauge the effect of his words. As if I suddenly had a double, I saw myself, standing still in the middle of the kitchen. My apron is dirty, I thought. This morning, putting it on to begin doing the housework, I saw on the front red traces of tomato juice and big greasy rings. I should have taken my apron off when I heard him open the door; it was the only thought that crossed my mind. Very thick, viscous silence settled in between us, and an acid reflux burned in my throat. Behind the closed windows, the sun sent rays that came crashing down on the waxed periwinkle blue cloth which covered the table. I certainly looked stupid with my arms just hanging there, my hands still wet, saturated with a sharp odor of bleach that he had to smell. A woman's scent, smell of ordinary mornings, just before cooking smells come to supplant it.

You only got what you wanted, right, I left it up to you. His voice crossed the space between us, got lost in a sort of fog and only came to me with great difficulty. But it got to me and it found its way to what remained of my consciousness, since I heard his words and I understood them. A buzzing suddenly invaded the room. I thought for an instant that a blue bottle fly was flying around above me. Carrion flies, that's what I call them. I wanted to raise my arm to swat it, but my arm no longer obeyed me. The buzzing grew louder and louder. But maybe it was the silence that was becoming intolerable.

He picked up the keys again that he had laid on the table when he put down the papers. Right now, he is going to go out of the kitchen, he is going to cross the hall and open the front door. I pictured each one of his gestures, the number of steps, eight in all to reach the threshold, I had counted them so many times, and the noise of a slammed door already resounded in my ears before he even made a move. But he stayed standing across from me. He was certainly waiting for something, but what? I tried to ask him why he did not leave right away, but with that, too, my voice stayed stuck in the back of my throat and a bizarre sound escaped my lips, something like a gurgle or a moan. That must have surprised him, he must have thought I was going to cry or scream, I don't know.

I thought of a statue, a stone statue, and I abruptly understood. That's it, I told myself, I am petrified. I was happy to have found the word. Petrified. Petrified. It pounded at my temples, decomposed into three syllables which pounded, pounded at the painful lining of my skull. Until now, I didn't know what that really meant. You're still standing but nothing more in you is alive. You no longer control anything. A connection problem between neurons and synapses, or so it seems. You have the distinct feeling that your blood has frozen. Your feet, your legs are stuck to the ground, no, not stuck, sealed. A muffled far-off beating comes to you, that seems to emerge from your center, but you know that it is only an echo from the time when you were still living, a few minutes earlier. Yet, I still waited. Both of us were waiting, since he wasn't leaving. I tried to calculate, to reason, I held on to words, numbers, numbers are solid, their logic has been tested. Implacable. I let myself be caught up in words, expressions, which tried to cling to the emptiness that was in me before falling, the echo of which was filling my head, one two buckle my shoe, three four open the door, a nursery rhyme which comes back from my earliest childhood memory, and which . . . For a minute, no, a few seconds, five, ten, twenty, I thought he was going to advance. That no longer meant anything, I knew, but a crazy hope, completely crazy, unreasonable, spun in my head and made me dizzy, and I thought, and if I collapsed now, right here, before him, paralyzed . . . hospital and all the rest. He would have to. And I watched the whole movie in my head. First my legs give way, followed by my body, in slow-motion, and I fall. He would hurry forward to catch me. He would only have an unstringed puppet in his arms, and maybe have not enough strength, or only really not enough desire to touch me to prevent me from crashing to the ground. The image of a bird struck by lightning in midflight suddenly crossed my mind. I lifted my head again, to see if.

What I read in his gaze, I can't explain it to you, but that's what got my blood flowing again. I felt a wave, an intense heat that was coming up from deep within me. Abruptly everything fell into place again. Everything became clearer. With sharp clarity. I reclaimed the place. A more intense brightness outlined each object, each piece of furniture. I was in my kitchen with a man. A man whom I knew so well that I could, at this very instant, only by looking at him, guess the dismay he was feeling. Yes, I know that may seem surprising, but it was apparent. He was uneasy. Big drops of sweat popped out on his forehead and on his lips. He had scarcely met my gaze when he turned his head away. As usual. He doesn't know how to look people in the eye. Always evasive. Before, in the time when . . . oh, how I loved the way he seemed to not want to linger over things or people, his detached, terribly charming demeanor. But the most troubling thing was that he had something about him that resembled fear, an infinitesimal glint in his eyes, barely perceptible, but right there, yes, a sort of apprehension like the one you feel when faced with a situation that you can't control. That's it. I suddenly understood. He hadn't expected that. I mean this total lack of reaction, or at least this sudden stillness that could make him think that I was impassible, yes, too calm for his liking. The calm before the storm. He could think that

I hadn't really understood what he was telling me. Whatever it was, he really seemed disconcerted. He probably expected more resistance. So, I still had this capacity to. He had to have prepared himself at length before coming to find me. Assured of his power over me, he must have predicted his replies, his convictions, my questions, his answers, my certain despair. Maybe even screams, pleas. He vented everything, without preliminaries. Next, he sorted everything out, and in the end, he struck me down: you have to learn to live with it. And, to force the nail in deeper, he continued, he spelled out the consequences, the logical consequences, the irrefutable argument. What did he say exactly? Oh yes! I left it up to you! And better yet, he added: it's what you wanted. Very skillfully, I have to admit that. So, I am the one who. Yes, everything went as expected, perhaps he even planned to expand on his indictment in the same manner. That's why it didn't come right out. I wondered if I shouldn't just let him go all the way through his act, he seemed so convinced that he had every right to! In listening attentively, respectfully to him, I would probably have helped him to get rid of this discomfort that my unpredictable behavior had created in him. I had thwarted his plans. Had he been rehearsing? Had he been advised by his new masters, the ones who knew the Law as he liked to repeat, and who knew that he needed to throw back all the responsibilities onto me and those like me, like getting rid of a heap of trash? Of course, it's a foolproof, tested strategy. They feel lighter that way, innocent, in full possession of their means, totally within their rights in the eyes of men—and especially in the eyes of God. But tell me, have we ever seen men feel guilty? The only guilty parties are women who refuse to submit to the laws. Clearly I could not claim a victim status.

I took two steps, I leaned on the wall across from the window. But he only appeared to me in shadow. And I wanted to see him. So I took two other steps in the direction of the door. He must have thought I was coming toward him and he recoiled, oh, just slightly, but I detected it. On the sink, very near me, a ray of sunlight shone off the blade of the knife, which I had used the night before, to cut the meat for dinner. I had set it there while doing the dishes. He met my gaze, looked away. The same thought crossed our minds, at the same moment. His expression changed. It was . . . it was scorn . . . I think. He knows me well. He shrugged his shoulders. He looked away.

And in this instant, what does the heroine do? What does the script dictate? Irresistibly attracted to the blinding flash of the blade that seems to be placed there by one of those chances which recalls fate, she extends her hand, he has his back turned, he can't see what's happening behind him, she seizes the knife, now he is in the hallway, she follows him, not very close behind, trying to make the least noise possible; the darkness in the hallway, the sudden madness which can engender despair, somewhere a child's cry, maybe in one of the bedrooms, everything seems to push her to accomplish the fatal movement, and she raises her hand.

A child's cry. Why did this expression nestle at the heart of the scene that I saw in my mind's eye? Had I really heard the child screaming? I stopped on the threshold. He too had stopped, all ears. I crossed the hall. I passed him quickly, without looking at him, I opened the bedroom door. The bed was still unmade. In the cradle, the child was flailing, tangled in the sheets. Red-faced, she let out angry little screams. When I bent over her, she quieted, her eyes glued on my face. I gently untangled her. I took her in my arms. She let a long sigh escape her lips before snuggling against my shoulder, her eyes still fixed on me. He was standing in the middle of the bedroom. He had followed me. He didn't make the slightest movement toward the child, his daughter.

Yes I know, I shouldn't have. I shouldn't have told him to get out. Not that way. That's not the way to speak to a man, even when he puts murderous ideas into your head. But, believe me, in those moments, nothing remains of our centuries-old upbringing. I didn't understand why he was still there, why he had followed me all the way into the bedroom. Was this his way of making me understand that he had every right to? He had not come home for three days. These last weeks, he had often been absent, and with reason! Since our last argument, a violent altercation where I showed myself to be intransigent, unmoving, I was living totally cut off, I no longer even answered the telephone. A way of giving myself a reprieve before hearing what he had to say. A flash of hatred invaded me. He had come to officially inform me of his intentions. It was a done deal. Calmly. No screams, no tears. I had been well-behaved, contrary to his expectations. Now, he had nothing more to do here. And because he left it up to me . . . I held the child very tightly in my arms. Maybe she gave me the strength to start functioning again. I looked at her. She was frowning and wasn't taking her eyes off me.

Go away! I don't want to ever see you here again! I pointed my arm toward the door. Those were the first words I pronounced since he came in. My voice was unusually shrill. And especially uncontrollable.

Calmly, as if he hadn't heard me, he pulled a pack of cigarettes out of his pocket. He opened it, took out a cigarette, and headed to the kitchen, very familiar with the house. The box of matches was in its place, on the shelf above the burner. He struck a match and, in a long inhale, he lit his cigarette. From where I was, I could follow his every move. Then he sort of sneered. Without turning around, in a calm voice, he said, since you are taking it that way, you have seven days to clear out. You should read the papers . . . right there. He indicated the sheaf of papers that he had brought and put on the kitchen table.

That's when I heard it, this voice inside me, the voice of wisdom, of reason, shall we say. A voice that distinctly whispered to me, calm down, you have everything to gain by not rushing things so as not to hold him up, be reasonable, be reasonable, think about your child. I thought about my mother. About the others, about all the others before me. I had a weight on my shoulders and I had the weight of this little body lying very peacefully, totally relaxed in my arms. She kept looking at me, and I felt like she was making herself heavier, so that I would have to dig my heels into the ground. She seemed attentive, focused. She was not moving. I realized that I was swaying back and forth since I had taken her in my arms, as if to rock her. She was my life, my only reason for being. I had waited too long, years, before feeling her move inside me. They didn't have the right, no one had the right to hurt her. Nothing should happen to her. Ever. I was going to help her to grow up. And for that, for her, I had to learn first to fight with the only means that I still had at my disposal. Very limited means, but that left me with enough room to maneuver. I laid her back on the double bed, I surrounded her with pillows, and I reassured her with a smile.

It had to start somewhere. I rejoined him in the kitchen. I opened the window, without thinking. Probably because of the cigarette smell. The smoke floated in the light, in white, moving wisps, then spread out in graceful swirls, before dissipating toward the ceiling. I had the choice. In reality, several solutions were within my reach. He was right. An arid stretch, fraught with insurmountable obstacles, lay before me. A space bristling with indestructible walls, guarded by ruthless jailers. And then on the other side, there was another path to travel, a very narrow path, the one outlined for me by this man. And as long as he had not pronounced the magic words of repudiation, the ones that have the power to ravage an entire life and a lot more, two lives in this particular case, luck was on my side, I could still imagine tomorrows. I had to start playing my role, to utter the words that he was expecting from me. That I react as a sensible, virtuous woman, who is above all conscious of the uselessness of her revolt. First, to agree to hush everything that seethed within me. I took a deep breath before starting, and while I was speaking, I felt all my convictions fly to pieces, fling themselves every which way before being pulverized, pieces of broken glass, sharp shards, glass dust that filled the air I breathed, inflamed my chest, flayed my throat, and wanted to keep the words from coming to my lips. The words that were coming out of my mouth were not mine, and this woman who, now sitting on a chair, was looking at her husband and was calmly discussing, in the hope of convincing him of her capitulation, an unconditional surrender that he wanted, this woman inhabited by something stronger than her, she was no longer me.

He ended up sitting across from me. He held up his cigarette and looked at it consuming itself. I no longer know what I said. I think I must have talked for a long time. I was convincing, by turns blinded by despair and submissive. I cried too, that is exactly what they expect of a woman. The only thing missing was his string of prayer beads when he reminded me of my duty as a Muslim woman. I was listening to him, my head bowed. You see, what astonishes me a bit, is that he let himself be so easily convinced of my sudden docility, without even seeking to understand the reasons. It's when I added, after all, it's a big house, that he ripped up all the papers that he had brought and asked me to make him a coffee. When he finally pronounced your name, I even thought, yes, I remember, I said to myself, she's lucky to have such a pretty name, when I think about the one my father gave me, without even consulting my mother! Oh, how I hated you, for that too! And then, I'm going to make you smile, I thought that you were very fragile, very dainty, with almond-shaped eyes, very black hair. A bit like a Chinese woman, probably because of the books I had read. With my status as first wife, already a mother, I saw myself reign over you, and over all the others that could follow you here. Glory to the concubines! A foretaste of paradise, or so men say. In good faith, on my honor! It was only a question of accommodation, of schedules, of equally shared rights and duties. Oh, by the way, do you know that he asked me to follow him into the bedroom, after, and that he took me, just like that, in broad daylight, right in this bed, in the morning light, with the child that he had put back in her cradle, and who did not take her eyes off of us? Didn't I ever tell you? And I opened up under him, and I moaned, softly, he almost cried with pleasure. I didn't even think about taking off my apron.

And don't you think it would be good if we got up now? Come here, let me brush your hair my sweet, red-haired daughter of Satan, and hurry up and get dressed, it won't be long before he's home.

IMPROVISATIONS

A middle-aged woman comes forward onto the stage. She seems to hesitate, takes a few steps back, exchanges a few words with someone in the wings, then comes back and abruptly engages with the audience:

"So, what do you think of me? *She twirls, smiles, moves toward the house. She looks at the silent audience and shrugs her shoulders.* Of course, you can't please everyone. Short term, for me, it means not to displease too much. Oh! If you had known me about . . . um . . . *she hesitates, casts a backward glance as if she were looking back at her past* only a few years ago. For those of you who want more details, I can add that in 'a few' there's a number with . . . two digits. *She speaks directly to someone in the house:* there, does that work for you, sir? Rest assured; I do not intend to annoy you with my buried youth. I try to get it back, every day, over and over, but it goes fast . . . it goes so fast. I'm a little out of breath now. But I'm still sturdy, look! *She makes a few pretty clumsy movements then stands still, as if she just realized she is ridiculous. She remains silent for an instant, then starts to speak again. Now, she speaks as if to herself.* Be yourself, that's what they told me! Speak, express yourself freely! Don't hesitate to show all the facets of your personality. You will not be judged on what you say, but on how you say it . . . Easy to say with all these people looking at me! Well, improvise! You have twenty minutes. Above all, no silences. Fill the time without giving the impression that you are filling it. *She looks around.* But there is nothing here. A bare set. They didn't tell me. They could have put a little effort into the scenery! There are no . . . armchairs, no bed . . . With a bed, you can improvise, you can invent anything, stories about love,

about death, or . . . in a corner, a concealed side door through
which to escape, in the theater you can always leave the stage
and then . . . yes, here for example an armoire full of those
secret drawers that you always end up opening, never in time,
with a mirror inside. A big mirror that appears as soon as you
open the door. A mirror to go back in time . . .

*She goes to the side of the stage, makes a move as if to open
a door and positions herself across from the alleged mirror.*
"Here . . . *she backs up a few steps while continuing to look
at herself in the mirror.*
"Here I am. In all my former glory. My hair . . . *she caresses
her head, straightens up.* My queenly demeanor. Before the
wreck. And my lips . . . *she tenderly outlines their shape with
her fingertips, closing her eyes.* My lifeboat red with desire, or
so he used to say. And my breasts, *she cups her hands under
her breasts* how did they put it, all those who took this path . . .
hills and valleys, tight, firm and dense. *She lifts up a corner
of her skirt, high enough* Gazelle, my amber-eyed Gazelle . . .
*she lowers her head and continues at length, as if reluctantly
stopped in her tracks. She corrects herself. She continues more
firmly.* Well, all of that's really nice, but I'm going to catch
cold if I keep this up. There's a draft, don't you feel it? It's just
that we never know which way the wind is blowing. I have
to be careful. Nothing more annoying than catching a cold.
Well, where I'm from we say 'to be hit by the wind.' Not a
bad expression, right? Ah! Because I haven't told you yet. I'm
not from here. Well, I wasn't born here. Did you guess that?
Hum . . . Surprise, surprise! I hope this won't impact the turn of
events . . . because that's what everyone tells me, really, you
wouldn't think you were Arab . . . your complexion, your
hair . . . oh, really? Random chance genetic combinations,
you know . . . mixtures . . . Berber, Vandals, Phoenicians, Arabs,
Turks, Spaniards, French . . . to keep this genealogy straight . . .
these cross-fertilizations . . . Well . . . looking at it closely, I can't
say. But like this, just the way I am, I could pass for . . . for a
Mediterranean woman, that's all! And I speak French, without
an accent. And I even know how to read and write! *She bursts*

out laughing. No, no, I'm not kidding, wait, I'll tell you everything. *Confidentially.* I wasn't born on this side of the Mediterranean. And neither was my mother. Nor was my father. My
father was named Ali. And my mother, Zahra, *she spells out:*
Z, A, H, R, A, pronunciation of the H is optional, too difficult
for you. It means flower. Something like Rose, Violet, or Daisy.
All first names mean something at home, in my country back
there as the other guy says. Me, I'm, well, I was . . . night . . .
Leïla, shadows and velvet . . . darkness and silence, well, I'm
talking about the first name that they gave me . . . over there . . .
I would have preferred to be light, Nour . . . but that too . . .
and I took the second L out of my name, one less L, gives me
wings, and it becomes Léïa, it's a better bet here. Introductions
are over.

*She stops, leans in toward the house as if to listen to someone
who might have called out to her . . .*

"What did I come here to do? In France? No? Really! Here,
you mean, right here, on this stage? To audition for the role of
course, to try my luck! It seems that I'm a born actress, who
asks nothing more than to blossom. In every role. A prodi-
gious capacity to mimic, essential for survival, especially on
foreign . . . land . . . *she takes a paper from her pocket and begins
to read* 'Amateur theater troupe seeks a thirty- to forty-year-
old woman, appearance rather fragile, free right away.' That's
what the ad said, right? They didn't even specify: experience
required. And what's more, I look the part. I know that because I read the whole play that they want to produce. Entirely
me, this character, tell me again, what's her name? Nora, yes,
that's it, *she croons,* Nour, Nora, Nour, Nora. I recognized
myself right off. I know . . . it's what every woman who came
here must say to you, well anyway . . . I'm not going to tell
you that I was just passing through by chance, that I came in
and that . . . as you seemed to be sitting there, quite comfortably
waiting for something, I didn't want to miss the chance to do
my act. The big time in the spotlight. *She chuckles.* No, enough
kidding around. I've been through this before, you certainly
noticed. I always play-acted. Nonstop, like every woman. Since
I was very small . . . compelled to . . . Here, when they said: go

ahead, it's your turn, I wasn't ready. The truth is, I prepared
nothing. I wasn't expecting to see such a crowd for an audition. *She assumes an affected tone* I hesitated so much between
Phèdre and Antigone that . . . Mediterranean women, too, you
probably noticed. But about the fragility issue . . . *she declaims
with emphasis:*

'And Phèdre gone down with you in the labyrinth
Would be with you found or lost . . .'

"Yes, that's just it . . . and there you have it. *She makes
a piteous gesture* This has a strange effect on people, these
lights, this silence, this expectation . . . *she moves toward back-
stage* The actresses are getting ready for tonight's play. That's
what they told me in the wings. *She leans over toward the house
and speaks in a low voice* You have to hang in there, it seems
that these are only women's stories. Because when women take
the floor, they are not ready to give it back. Here's proof . . .
we say women who make a fuss . . . we never say: men who
make a fuss. Is it because men don't make fusses? Or is it because they make history, the real one? Women's stories . . .
there are so many of them . . . I really wonder if . . . I could
also . . . but no . . . If only they had given me a word, only one,
I could have put it through the hole in the needle, threaded it,
and begun to sew right then . . . Penelope at her work. Another Mediterranean woman . . . While we're waiting . . . Too
late, I have no choice now. Hey, there is an interesting word,
what do you think? Choice. Choice. *Bombastically* To have
or not to have the choice . . . The choice to live or not to. The
choice to keep going or to go away. To choose to venture into
the labyrinth, to find or to lose yourself . . . *she points her
finger at a few people seated in the front row* You there, and
you . . . You didn't choose to come here to listen to me, it's
your job, but you can now choose not to hire me. To get up and
to tell me to leave. And on my end, can I choose to go away?
There's still time . . . but . . . *she sighs* Every choice implies a
renunciation. Risks. One above all, the one where you make
a mistake, regret . . .

She turns away, takes a few steps backward. A voice booms.
'You still have 15 minutes!'
She comes back slowly downstage.

"To choose to come into the world . . . that, is the end of the thread. We do not choose to come into the world on a sunny morning or a stormy night. To be born on one side of the Mediterranean or on the other. No more than we can choose our skin color or a mother's smile. My mother . . . the least we can say is, she didn't choose to bring me into the world. It seems that she even tried everything to keep me from seeing the light of day. Potions, hot baths, gymnastics, somersaults, maybe even knitting needles, who knows . . . all the tricks they had up their sleeves at that time . . . but it's entirely conceivable that I was already strong-willed. Maybe I had already chosen *she stresses the word* to hang in there. Those are the stories she used to tell, the ones that rocked me to sleep as a child. Something to give me a good start in life! But don't go thinking that I hold it against her. I would have certainly done the same thing in her place. Sometimes she even happened to give birth twice in the same year, in January and in December. A good average, right? More of an egg-layer than a mother hen. Easy to lose count . . . and especially when the scale leans dangerously toward the girl's side and you have to try to regain balance! Of course, children are God's blessing, it's a good way to keep husbands, and it keeps them busy enough to prevent them from looking elsewhere . . . but at that pace, you wonder if God is not too bountiful, too generous with some . . . but . . . truth be told it wasn't because of that that my mother was not happy . . . hey, there's another interesting word . . . 'happy' . . . especially when it describes women . . . we could spend hours exploring the changeable and circumstantial definitions of this word . . . To get back to my mother, I think the reason she held it against us so much was that she could not even choose the color of one of her dresses, the face of the man who shared her life, her children's names, a soap's fragrance, the words to tell herself . . . picture it a little, not being able to choose whose hands will caress you, not being able to choose to open your eyes in the morning or to keep on dreaming or even to let yourself be softened by an evening's sweetness. I don't even know if she had time to dream. *She hums:*

"'Back when life was so beautiful . . . memories and regrets too . . .'"*

"I suppose she loved us anyway. In her own way . . . how to put it? A bit animal-like . . . she protected us, took care of us when we were sick, gave us something to eat when we were hungry. A slap at random, from time to time, to the boy or the girl who got in the way, in order to balance, or to not lose control of the situation. That's quite enough to raise a bunch of kids, right? Not even the time to smile or to watch us grow up . . . That's the thing I missed the most, a mother's smile and her attentive gaze. When I saw the other mothers smile, the ones who came to pick up their children when school got out . . . when I saw their eyes light up when . . . that's why I chose not to be like her. Not even a little bit. Ever. That's the choice that determined all the others.

She abruptly turns toward the alleged mirror. She puts her hair up and looks at herself worriedly. She runs her hand over her forehead, as if to smooth it.

"But . . . there the creases are . . . the same as hers. And my eyes, you'd say . . . the spitting image . . .

In a wrathful gesture she puts her hands on each side of her face, as if to erase the wrinkles at the corners of her mouth.

"At my age she already had *she counts on her fingers* five, no six children, and sometimes a miscarriage here and there, this one's a miss, she used to say jubilantly . . . a deformed body, nothing feminine anymore, no . . . and still, she kept on . . . seven, eight . . . until death followed. On this one, I'm talking about my father. As for him, he couldn't keep up the pace, still . . . He ended up just letting go. Too hard. He couldn't bear to see us swarming around him. And anyway, he didn't do much, at least around the house. Typical, he was a man. With a big . . . mustache. That's the only thing I really remember. We didn't dare look him in the eyes. So we stared at his

---

* From *"Feuilles mortes,"* a poem by Jacques Prévert that was later set to music. — *Trans.*

mustache. And we knew how to interpret the slightest quiver. We used to call it atmospheric disturbance. That was the household weather. Reports with no danger of error. It often hailed . . . you had to wait for it to pass. In silence. Even the boys got out of the way then. And my mother took it all in silence. The storms, the squalls, between the too infrequent lulls. Now you understand why I left, why I raised anchor. *She hums,* 'I left my country, I left my sun . . .'"

She stops. She waits. A voice booms, 'Five-minute warning!'

"Hey, I thought I was done. Well, I only have to keep on going. Where was I? What did the ad say? Oh yes, 'Seeking a fragile woman . . .' Why? What does fragile mean? Submissive and soft? The exact opposite of a domineering woman or a shrew? *She assumes an ironic tone* A dainty woman, and weak, so weak . . . weak enough to make men want to protect her! *She chuckles* Nothing less fragile than a woman, that's what I say! But we can, we know how to pretend really well, how to fake docility, fragility, orgasm . . . so convincingly that men only get fired up. And that does them so much good to feel strong, to believe themselves to be the dispensers of pleasure . . . About fragility, so, *she turns towards the wings,* can I sit down now?

Her eyes search for a seat. From the wings, someone hands her a stool. She settles down.

"Phew! That's better. Where was I? I'm repeating myself, I'm sorry. Oh yes, I left one day. I couldn't stand looking at the mustache of every man around me. The most obvious . . . sign of virility.

She gets up, puffs out her chest, stands still in an attractive pose and says, making her voice serious,

"I am a Man, with a capital *M* and a mustache. Make way, make way, let me through! *She lets herself fall back on the stool* And there you have it. For a long time, I looked for a man without a mustache.

She hides her face in her hands. Her body shakes with tremors, we don't know if she is laughing or crying. The stage

---

*From the song *"Adieu mon pays"* by Enrico Macias, 1962. He was a *pied-noir* exile and sings about the nostalgia he feels for Algeria. — *Trans.*

darkens. She rises and speaks, with her back to the audience.
Men, I found some! Not just one. Several. And I didn't pick
them either. I let myself get carried away by . . . let's say . . .
how things turned out. I left everything behind, the storms, the
squalls, the sun, yes, I sailed for a long time before coming to
you. I've known wrecks . . . oh! the fragile skiff on troubled
seas . . . and I survived . . . carried away by the desire to throw
off everything that was weighing me down.

*She sits on the ground, at center stage, curls up her knees and
puts her arms around them.*

"Untying all the strings that were holding me back, one by
one, throwing the memories overboard, the too intense taste of
the seasons, the looks, the smell of the jasmine flowers and the
women's songs in the night, of the too bright light on the white
terraces, the shouts of the water carrier and the murmur of
the fountains in the squares. And to tell it like it is, I
succeeded . . . well . . . almost . . . at the risk of . . . there is a specific word to say that at home . . . an untranslatable word . . . to
specify those who no longer have souls, no more roots, no more
memory, who look for all the ways to make people forget and
to forget themselves who they are, who believe that they will be
accepted by others this way, at the risk of losing themselves . . .
but I forgot this word . . . even this . . .

*Followed by a long silence. Then she shakes it off and rises,
facing the audience.*

"That's all, for the nostalgia bit. Pathetic, right? I hope you
enjoyed it. You want more? I can go on . . . make you laugh or
make you cry. Your choice. You just have to ask. You just have
to put on the mask, to make your voice heard and everybody
believes it. Here, now I'm going to . . ." *the stage manager's
voice booms,*

"Thank you, madam, before you go leave your contact information, and we will contact you if necessary."

She backs up a few steps, slowly, visibly tired.

"Oh, it's over now . . . yes, time's gone by . . . the actresses
are certainly just about to . . . very well . . . then, *speaking to the
audience* . . . enjoy the show . . . maybe see you soon."

IF, ON A SUMMER'S NIGHT . . .

Here is my language,
necklace of stars around the necks of the ones I love.

—Mahmoud Darwich,
"A Rhyme for the *Muallaquâi*"

"Sleep eludes me. I do not know why. I want . . . I want to play," whispers Leïla to Aziza, who is lying right next to her. "It's past midnight. Why don't we go up to the terrace, to consult the stars?"

Lost in her customary dreams, Aziza does not answer right away. After a long minute, she ends up coming back to the world and sits up straight.

"Who's coming with us?" continues Leïla, in a louder voice.

"Me!" cries out Amina.

"Me too," says Warda, who turns toward the languid Assia, on the brink of sleep. She tells her,

"Listen! Come here, can't you hear the slow murmur of the waves licking the shoreline? The night is ideal, you'd say that it was holding its breath expectantly. Do you think that we could knock on destiny's door tonight?"

Seized by a sudden exaltation, she rises. As if to better convince them to join in the game, she pulls the curtains aside, opens the window, and limps toward her youngest sister.

"Look up and watch! There is a full moon, the brightness coming down from the sky is overwhelmingly sweet. Do you want, tell me, do you want us to go further than dreams? Let's go, before the final sigh of night, let's go join dawn together before the gazes of men dissipate its softness."

Still and quiet, Selma listens to this strange exhortation, each word of which stands out and vibrates for a long time in the silence of the night. She hesitates for an instant. She too would like to know what will be the pattern of her tomorrows, but she dreads having to face the mysteries of destiny. Forever wise, forever submissive, perhaps even before opening her eyes to the world, vaguely sensing that there would be no place for happiness, not even a few crumbs, for her, the seventh daughter, she, who came into the world, one winter evening, welcomed by anger, tears, and affliction.

The delicate Naïma, whose family unanimously agrees when they say that all the fairies blessed her birth, the beauty who seemed already to be sleeping, stretches voluptuously. She holds Amina back by the arm, who was readying herself to slip out of her bed,

"Wait for me, I'm coming with you."

Suddenly, life is reborn in the bedroom's semi-darkness. One can hear furtive feet tread, jingling, the wrinkling of sheets as they are thrown off, stifled laughter, then steps that scarcely disturb the stillness of this summer night. As careful as Indians, they half-open the door, cross the long dark corridor, and, one after the other, climb the stairs leading to the terrace. A delicious coolness welcomes them and they slowly soak in the exquisite sensation.

Now here they are: seven young women, seven sisters clothed in light white veils, so light that they resemble wings that their combined desire unfurls. Seven young women standing on the hills of their old dwelling, facing the sea. They go to meet their destiny. They hold hands and contemplate the sky.

From the gazelle, Aziza gets a timid look and a delicate step. Reserved by nature, she seems always to feel withdrawn, probably due to the fear that an unchecked stroke will reach her at the heart of her extreme solitude. Still, she is the one who in this instant comes forward first while Leïla ties a knot in her handkerchief, pronounces her name and slowly recites the words that can open the doors of the night.

> "Oh you,
> Spirits of the night
> Whose breaths rekindle the embers

That glow red at the heart of darkness,
Could you give us a sign
To light the way
And unveil what is written for her?"

In the night's tranquil transparency shot through with long slivers of moon, they collect themselves, presently attentive to the least noise. Seeming to erupt from the sky, a far-off rumble comes to them, which they try to recognize. Bit by bit, the roar becomes clearer.

"A plane," cries out Leïla, "it's a plane! You're going to leave, I'm sure of it, one day you will cross the oceans, you will go away on board a steel bird." Warda interrupts her,

"Here's what the prophecy says: the one who will come toward you will lead you far, very far from us. You will live in countries where the winters are white and long, very long. You will forget the summers and the light sprouting up from between the jasmine flowers. There, far from us, you will try in vain to collect the fragrances of dawns and the sweetness of dusks, without ever being able to rediscover the flavor."

Aziza grows quiet. Tears come to her eyes while her sister invents an exile with a bitter taste for her.

Selma comes toward her, takes her by the arm, and pulls her to the edge of the terrace.

"Don't listen to a word she says! She is a poet, you know that, and like every poet, she has the strange and fascinating compulsion to let herself be too easily carried away by the magic of words, to let them flow out of her without ever looking to hold them back, believing thus to act on the ugliness of the world. If such is your destiny, you will perhaps leave, you will discover other worlds, other landscapes, places so beautiful, so alive that they will make you forget the grayness of days spent behind closed doors."

Very near to them gushes a clear bold voice, brimming with laughter or tears, the voice of Amina the rebel, the one whose excesses, demands, and angry outbursts too often upset the too strict prescriptions for the day.

"My turn now! Leïla, tie another knot in your handkerchief!

A very tight, very solid knot, so that what has to be may be revealed."

While Leïla pronounces the venerated incantation, a strong gust rises, an abrupt swirl that makes the surrounding doors and windows slam and raises an acrid and fine dust that whirls around all of the assembled young women, obliges them to cover their faces with their hands and to close their eyes.

Aziza has moved away. She curls up in the darkest corner; she melts into the shadow and seems to want to withdraw herself from the game. A sudden worry squeezes her heart. What will become of my beloved sister? The stirrings, the torments, the storms are what await her. What breath of wind will carry her off? What dream will take her away from us? Will she be able to resist the dark forces that come to slander her every once in a while? Will she one day be able to drop her weapons and let them clip her wings?

At the same time, as if to face an abruptly unleashed nature, her arms outstretched, her body given, Amina dances and takes off the veils that hinder her. Her slender and fragile silhouette seems to challenge the powerful sea breeze, in her grace, her unfettered step, the harmonious amplitude of her movements seem to answer every question, to quiet all the rumors only to leave space for the fire burning within her.

Now Selma is the one who has to stand. Selma, the wild secret child, the one who to better fade into the background has made armor out of her silences and a rampart that protects her from others out of her dreams, and especially from herself.

Without consulting each other, they all come toward her, surround her, brush her with their joined hands, unfold around her a zone of tenderness, thus perhaps attempting to reach the place where lies the first pain forever rooted in her being.

"Do you want, tell me, do you want to share these instants with us, do you want to for once link your dreams to ours and listen to the hymn of the night?"

Warda's voice is soft, very soft, she wants it to appease, and Selma surrenders bit by bit to the nocturnal serenity. Leïla bends over and makes a third knot in her handkerchief. She casts the long incantation skyward.

For a long moment, nothing moves. They try to lend an ear to discern a quiver, a rustle, the least luminous or sonorous sign that they could translate, they tried feverishly, impatiently to scrutinize the sun, only an absolute silence answers their expectation.

"There! There! I saw it! A shooting star! Quick, make a wish before it shatters on the land or in the sea!"

Assia, standing on her tiptoes, her arm outstretched, indicates a point in the vastness of the sky. She vigorously shakes her sister who does not react.

"*I* didn't see anything," answers Selma sadly. "Your imagination is playing tricks on you, as usual!"

They all exclaim at the same time.

"Yes, there, it disappeared now, but it was really a shooting star! We saw it! It's for you, it's a sign, a message! Oh yes! You can ask for what you want, and heaven will grant it!"

Touched by their insistence, by a solicitude that she knows intended to give her some hope, Selma smiles and joins in the game.

"I want . . . I want to go too, go to discover other worlds where I can finally give free reign to the innumerable desires that fill me in vain with turmoil. And first things first . . ."

Her voice breaks, then she collects herself, and in an almost inaudible whisper she adds:

"No, no, to be loved by all. Simply. That's my wish."

"Love, love, there, the word has finally been said," trumpets Naïma.

She repeats the word, lets it slam in the silence, like a challenge.

"It's with love that I too want to fill my life, to the brim! Leïla, my turn now, I want to know: who will come to deliver me? In a plane or in a boat, on a white horse or in a nice car, whatever, I've been waiting for him for such a long time. Let him come! And above all, let him enter into this dwelling his arms full of gifts! And then . . . wait, I forgot an important detail: let him be handsome, if not . . . it is not worth him troubling himself!"

A general burst of laughter greets her words.

"And if he comes on foot, in sandals?" replies Assia maliciously, "you aren't going to open the door?"

Naïma assumes an air of false disdain and shrugs her shoulders.

"Wait, wait, you'll see! Go on, Leïla, my turn!"

Amused, Leïla obliges. First a fourth knot in the handkerchief, then she names the chosen one and solemnly recites the spell, full of emphasis. Very quickly they perceive the whirr of a motor followed by a squeal of brakes quite nearby. They hurry to the edge of the terrace; a car just turned at the street corner. They scarcely had the time to glimpse its taillights.

"I told you so," comments Naïma soberly, "he was in such a hurry, didn't you see? So much of a hurry that I didn't even have time to see if it was a nice car! Too bad!"

Warda, silent for a moment, seizes Leïla by the arm.

"I'll skip my turn. I who expect no one, and whom no one expects, I know where to find the keys. I know where to draw the strength to accomplish my destiny. It is up to me to untangle the threads. No need to interrogate the stars. Has anyone ever seen a creature such as me escape from what, the instant that I was conceived, has determined my entire existence? The only thing I have of my childhood is the memory of a long, lonely and difficult crossing. Now, I also know how to read the looks full of pity of those who come up to me, and that's enough for me. But there are other symbols, essential to my life, the symbols that opened up for me, and will continue for a long time I hope, to leave all paths open to me. It's thanks only to them that I am alive, that I go forward with my head held high and that I can forget or make up for all the deficiencies of nature. Do you know that when I read, when I write, when I let the words come to me, all that surrounds me disappears? And Warda the cripple, poor Warda, the inaptly named, can thus imagine taking possession of the world and molding it in her way."*

She quiets for an instant, then in a chuckle that resembles a sob, she begins again.

---

* *Warda* means rose and, by extension, refers to all flowers. — *Author*

"And even if I don't know how to dance, no one will ever be able to keep me from believing that it's for me that the poet wrote: '*I stretched a cord from star to star and I dance.*'"[*]

Deeply upset by the confession of this immense distress whose ravaging effects she had sensed, Leïla takes her in her arms. She feels this restive body, which stiffens in the refusal of all compassion, tremble against her.

Gently, Warda disentangles herself and grabs the handkerchief that Leïla clutches in her hands.

"Let me call on the spirits, I'm going to do it for you. I only hope that they will listen to me as they have listened to you."

Even before she has finished pronouncing the incantation's last words, a child's cry pierces the silence of the night. They all hear it very distinctly. Without surprise. Leïla is not only the eldest sister, she is also the one who very quickly and very often seconded, if not replaced, the mother too busy to give them the attention which they needed to grow up. No one knows better than her how to console, to listen to, to comprehend, to calm, to comfort, to encourage. It is to her side, like Warda at this moment, that they come for refuge each time they hurt, and patiently, delicately, she dresses their wounds, without ever daring to tell herself that they stole her childhood, without ever thinking about revolt or complaint.

Before even one of them has time to make a comment, she takes back the handkerchief and calls Assia.

"Come, come quickly, before daylight comes to chase away the spirits of the shadows, quickly, it's your turn now."

With an assured step, Assia comes forward to the center of the terrace. Without real curiosity, she awaits the prophecy that will confirm for her what she already knows. Her dreams and desires have a face, a name, a presence that accompanies her all day long. Her path has been preordained, she has known it from the moment when, upon leaving high school, she exchanged glances with Mourad. Her life is nothing more than a succession of stolen moments in doorways, of messages exchanged in the greatest secrecy, yet with the complicity of her

---

[*] Federico García Lorca. May also refer to Arthur Rimbaud. —*Author*

sisters. She is the first and only one among them to discover the excitement and trances of love that Naïma has just so ardently invoked. She is only seventeen, and she still has to wait a long time, but who cares. With every passing day, she comes closer to this happiness that she awaits with all her innocent strength; it is a certainty deeply rooted within her.

As if to echo this fervor, the first flashes of the sun abruptly illuminate the horizon and cover the surface of the water with iridescent shimmers. The air is filled with a still misty brightness that bit by bit chases away the shadows of the night.

The seven sisters now stand facing the sea. They hold hands and contemplate the sky where the stars are being snuffed out. Then, in the same impulse, they turn away, cross the terrace and while the muezzin's powerful voice rises, they regain their bedroom and ready themselves to face the day.

ON A COMMA

Marie pursues me all the way to my dreams.

She appears in the middle of the night and does not leave me, until the crack of dawn.

In the fragile instant when you hesitate to go back to the edges very near to consciousness, I don't know who I am, where I am.

And then, dissipating all the images that haunt me, there is my mother's voice: "Sarah, wake up!"

Marie never completely disappears. It happens that as I read a word, she emerges in broad daylight, as present and unpredictable as in my dreams. It seems that I see her everywhere. She is sometimes standing at the street corner, right where she used to wait for her friends in the morning to go to the lycée, exactly at the corner of rue de Lyon and rue du Quatorze-juillet.

It was by questioning all the old neighborhood shopkeepers that I succeeded in identifying all the places that changed their names after independence. It is her, too, that I imagine, under a tree, standing against the Jardin d'essai's gates. At the exact spot where she met Jean-Paul, every evening coming back from the lycée. Or else, she jostles me, a laughing young woman with a sweet-tooth as she herself confessed, when I am in front of the door of the Poussin Bleu, the best pastry shop in Belcourt, the only one where the sign has not changed to this day.

As for Jean-Paul, I could recognize him in the middle of the densest crowd. I know everything about him. His way of walking, with his torso slightly bent forward, as if to make people forget about his height, one of a child grown up too quickly. His face with such dark coloring that he could have been taken for an Arab. His rebellious strand of hair, stiff with gel that very quickly fell back over his eyes *a deeper blue than a stormy sea.* He entered me through her words. I would recognize his voice, his musician's hands. Up until his smell, the Jean-Marie Farina lavender water with which he sprayed himself every morning, and also before each one of their dates. Sweet smell of lavender that in the evening permeated Marie's hair.

Marie's hair . . . In my dreams she appears to me with a halo of soft, blonde curls, her head circled in light. A golden helmet, like Simone Signoret, whose film was recently replayed on television. But it sometimes happens that in a graceful movement, she makes long locks of dark shiny hair swirl around her, in every way similar to mine.

I have to reread the notebook. To look carefully. It could be that some details escaped my attention. But is that really necessary? It is through Jean-Paul's words that Marie's face is drawn. Hence, Marie's eyes, *"eyes of wild grass made golden by the infinite rustle of the wind."*

I learned this phrase from Jean-Paul's letter by heart. A few others, too. Those that bring tears to my eyes, because I know no one will ever find such words to speak to me or to write to me. What a pity that Marie did not leave any letters other than this one! She must have taken them with her the day she left her house. Or perhaps she destroyed them before leaving. But I'm sure that she forgot none of the words, that they are printed in a corner of her memory. Maybe even now she repeats them to herself once in a while, just like that, when she is looking at herself in a mirror. So that she remembers the light of that gaze which transfigured her life.

Mama does not understand what is happening to me. I often feel her gaze fixed on me, as if she were looking at my face to find something that would have escaped her vigilance. The other day, she really tried. "You're changing, Sarah, you're not the same anymore." An observation which seems to astonish her. However, she knows quite well that I'm not her little girl anymore ever since the day that my father and she accepted the marriage proposal.

It's true, something has changed in me. I'm not alone anymore. And then, I just discovered that love really can exist.

Not only in films or in books. But that, she cannot see with her motherly eyes.

My mother's name is Meriem.

She is only two years younger than Marie.

I do not like to think of Marie with a woman's features, a woman who could resemble my mother. For me, Marie is eighteen. My age. And I'm the one she resembles. My mother is the first one I went to.

She's the one to whom I tried to ask all the questions that would have helped me to better understand Marie's story. She sometimes answers, but she doesn't understand my insistence and this desire I have to hear her tell stories about her youth. She must think that it's because the date set for my wedding is approaching. The desire to identify with her or else to hang on to my childhood. She's the one who found the notebook. A little ninety-six-page notebook, covered in green paper, hidden in the back of a closet in a storeroom, in the middle of a pile of old magazines kept by my grandmother, who never throws anything away. No one before me had ever read it.

Marie's story is there, in this abandoned or forgotten notebook, I will never know. It has, in these few pages, miraculously come to me.

"January 2nd, 1962: *what does this year have in store for me? war forever and always? Last night, well after midnight, I was woken up by several explosions, very close by. Plastic explosives again. I heard the ambulances' sirens. Mama came to check if Isabelle and I were asleep. As if we could sleep through all of that. It has been such a long time that we haven't been able to sleep the whole night. We wait, our eyes open, we wait for it to begin. I don't even jump when I wake anymore, I feel that I'm no longer afraid. She sat at my bedside and began to bring up the idea of a departure, once again. With 'ifs . . .' and tears in her eyes. She says that we cannot stay in this neighborhood anymore, that it is becoming too dangerous, especially for young women. That's also what Jean-Paul told me yesterday, when he left me near the Monoprix. He almost argued with a group of young people, Arabs, who were looking at me too*

*insistently. He is jealous! Oh joy! That, of course, flatters me, but
longing looks at me, that's not too unpleasant . . . and then they
all know me! He can't bear that a man other than him may notice
me, turn to look at me. He stayed standing there to watch them
as I went up the alley. I like that my street bears this name, allée
des Mûriers. You would think we were in a village. Right in the
heart of Algiers! But that would take a lot of imagination . . ."*

Allée des Mûriers. For us now, it's rue de Kaboul, from the
name of the mosque christened by those who invaded it. I was
even unaware that it bore this name. Mama remembers. She
showed me several postcards that were pretty old with this address on the back: 9, allée des Mûriers, Belcourt. Our address.

I can no longer bear men's looks, either. The avid eyes of all
the young people leaning with their backs against the walls
all day long. Still, they don't make comments when I pass in
front of them. Because I am from the neighborhood. *Bent el
Houma.* They also know that my brothers would not allow
them to disrespect me. But their looks are often even more
insolent and explicit than the words that they don't dare to
say aloud.

And the veil that I've worn for a few months, I'm sure, only
serves to exacerbate their imagination. On Fridays, I don't even
dare to leave my house. They are all posted in front of the
mosque door waiting for daily prayer. And locked in my room,
I relive Marie's Sundays.

"March 26, 1962: *it's midnight; after the concert of car
horns, the concerts of pots, silence has returned. A crazy day!
To say that a cease-fire had been signed a few days ago . . . And
ever since, you'd say that the rage and the violence have intensified, that there are no longer limits. They shoot down men in the
street as they would shoot down rabid dogs. I don't understand.
Jean-Paul could not come to our date. I waited for him out
in the sun for over an hour. The soldiers removed the crowd-
control barriers after the protest at plateau des Glières, but it
was too late. I had to leave before the returning protestors came
back down from Télelmy. There was quite a crowd, and traffic*

was blocked. I had to take a long detour. I came home late and I was in for one of Mama's scenes. The end of the war is unavoidable and men stubbornly keep up their madness. Here, in Belcourt, they are all preparing for the July 1st referendum. Some have even begun to make green and white flags with red stars and crescents in the middle. Aicha told me. But until then . . . Tomorrow is Sunday . . . Mama allowed me (we had to negotiate for a long time) to go out, in spite of everything. She is so upset by what is happening, so disoriented, that she did not even set any conditions. In a few hours I will be in your arms, Jean-Paul . . . good night my love . . ."

Marie's Sundays . . . The family walks on the sidewalks of rue de Lyon. The sunny paths of the Jardin d'essai, overrun with children's shouts, lovers' sighs, and the creaking of strollers.

The rue de Lyon is now called rue Belouizdad. Under the plane tree leaves in the Jardin d'essai, children and families are still there. Lovers too. But they hide.

They embrace; they separate at the least sound of steps, at the least whisper of wind in the leaves. At times they are even chased away by the gatekeepers or jeered at by children.

When I go shopping, I sometimes take a detour, without telling my mother, who only talks about the recent kidnappings of young women. I content myself with going through the gates and taking a few steps down the garden's main path, only a few minutes, the time it takes to imagine a boy's arm around my waist, his face leaning over me, a rebel strand of hair falling back into his eyes and the words he could say to me.

That's when I repeat that sentence of Jean-Paul's intended for Marie: *"In the evening, before I fall asleep, I close my eyes and let the light from our Sundays of clear water and secret foliage echo within me for a long time."*

"April 29, 1962: I haven't gone to the lycée for two weeks. All institutions of learning are closed or so they tell me. How long time seems to me! I live in wait. Most of my friends have already left. I don't even know if I should continue to study. Mama doesn't want me to go out anymore. She who was so

insistent that I take my Baccalaureate exam! I have not seen
Jean-Paul for over a week. I miss him so much! But the idea of
his departure is especially intolerable to me. Since our last meet-
ing, I can only think about the moment when we will separate.
In a few days, he will join his brother in Paris. His parents will
still stay here, the time to get ready to move. How will I be
able to breathe without him? Mama procrastinates. She doesn't
know where to go. She doesn't want to leave Algiers. She is
waiting to see how things turn out. It's her favorite expression.
She doesn't stop repeating it. She tries to hide from us that she
is afraid. But all it takes is one look at her. She is afraid of
the future, the unknown, and of the decisions that she will have
to make. She fears that her two dear daughters, Isabelle and I,
all that remains to her (her voice tearful at this exact instant)
will be one day taken hostage by those whose hard feelings
are sharpened by this war's horrible end. I try to tell her that
this is our neighborhood, that everyone here knows us, that the
neighbors promised to ensure our protection, it does no good.
She no longer trusts anyone. She only leaves the house to go to
the Mozabite grocers across the street. Her friend Zineb is un-
able to reassure her. She too is also very afraid for her husband
who works at the port. Every morning to go to the employment
center on the docks, he has to go through European neighbor-
hoods. And with all the attacks . . .
  Oh, Jean-Paul, to no longer hear death or hate spoken of!
How I would love to feel you close to me, to hear you endlessly
tell me that you love me, that war stops at Love's gates and that
nothing will be able to separate us!"

Exploding bombs. Nights and days interrupted by bursts of
machine-gun fire. Men who fall, who run every which way,
and women who howl looking for someone close to them.
The streets littered with corpses. From wherever she is, when
she sees the images of a present as terrible as her youth had
been, Marie surely must remember. She couldn't have forgotten.

I picked up my history books and notebooks again. I would
like to find the dates again, the names, the facts, to know what

happened during the few months when Marie was keeping her journal. But there is almost nothing about this period, between March 19, the day they signed the cease-fire following the Evian Accords, and July 5, "historic date of the day the country gained independence." Only two dates are mentioned: May 2, 1962, car bombing at the port of Algiers in front of the dockers' employment center and June 7, fire at the university library. I'll never know if Zineb's husband was counted as one of the sixty-two victims of the attacks at the port buried the next day. Marie doesn't mention it.

"May 3, 1962: *he left this morning. Yesterday we walked in the streets up to the operating field and we were no longer afraid of anything. I would have even liked to die in those instants, to die close to him, with his arms tight around me. When will we see each other again? I can no longer think about anything else. I only have words, his words, more luminous, softer than a spring dawn. He caressed my face for a long time. 'I want to keep the imprint of your smile in my hands, more precious than last rites.' My love, when will you be able to say those words to me again? This evening, in the silence of night, it's my turn now I want to let them penetrate me, slowly, adagio, you would say, you, the musician. May they invade all of me, may they join my heartbeats, become confused with my being and become my only reality. Hence, I will no longer be afraid of tomorrows without you.*"

Mama doesn't understand the reasons for the sudden interest that I show in our country's history. Or at least, in a very specific period of this history. I feel her annoyance at the too numerous questions I ask her. I get the impression that she doesn't want to talk about it too much because the wounds are reopened today.

So I keep quiet. I know that she too is afraid for us. She is astonished that I am not more interested in my trousseau, in my dresses, and she nags me about fittings at the dressmaker's. It's her most urgent preoccupation. There is of course my father, but I don't dare ask him for anything; we aren't used to broaching such subjects. In reality, we rarely say a word to each other! It's as if he wasn't there. So I seek refuge at my grandmother's side, and in her bedroom in the evening, only she consents to tell me the story of those days, a story filled with those turbulent moments that the most thorough, most well-documented of historians would not know how to retrieve. A history with a human face.

I could listen to her for hours. She searches far back in her memories to describe for me the disfigured town, divided by hatred and despair.

The Muslim neighborhoods. The European neighborhoods. The men posted at the barricades set up at the insurmountable borders of each one of these neighborhoods. Bitterly negotiated agreements. Coming out of a very different reality from the "historic" Evian Accords. The tense negotiations between the OAS and the FLN militants: let's exchange a European family residing in a Muslim neighborhood for a Muslim family residing in a European neighborhood. That is how my grandparents left their house to move in here. A hastily organized move by the militia from both camps. The arrival in Belcourt, a neighborhood mainly inhabited by Arabs, caught in a vise between two European neighborhoods, the Champ de manœuvre and the Ruisseau, just after the night shooting which had targeted their apartment, in the Ruisseau precisely. And then, these few meters to cross under high surveillance, in the no-man's-land, between the two barriers set up by the Jardin d'essai, a few meters when, for a brief instant, the two families crossed paths. And finally, their move—which they thought temporary—into the Sanchez house, Marie's house.

Marie abandoned her notebook that day.

I'm in her room. She used to lie on these same tiles on summer evenings, just under the open window. Inside the house, nothing has changed. The piano now out of tune is still in the same place. Only the windows were barred, and the outer wall was made at least two meters higher; the outline of the stone wall which surrounded the house and showed the garden is still visible. And when I sit here from where, at the beginning of their relationship, sitting on the front steps—her observation post—she was on the lookout for whole hours for Jean-Paul to come, I hear the street noises. But in the summer heat, the nights still exhale the lingering smell of honeysuckle and jasmine.

Each night, when I take up the notebook, when at night I listen to her voice which runs all the way along these pages yellowed in the shade of time and forgetfulness, in these words written with purple ink, it's as if Marie were here, beside me. It's true, I'm no longer alone. The breath of her love soaks slowly, gently into me, and my own life no longer seems only to be attached to the world by the tender and crazy rhythm of this long tragic lament.

"May 12, 1962: *I'm eighteen today. Nothing is more unbearable than this feeling of absence and emptiness that Jean-Paul's departure dug in me. I feel as if an essential part of my being has been amputated. I have no news of him. The mail is no longer distributed. We too are going to leave. Under the pressure of the events, Mama has resolved to leave the neighborhood. Everything speeds up. Madness of despair. We have to leave. Tomorrow, we will leave the house, this house where I was born. For our safety, they told us. All the people here want to get us far from this climate of hatred, a hatred more and more weighty, more and more visible, more and more difficult to contain. Yesterday, some rocket fire hit the market very close to us. I saw bloody bodies. I saw women on their balconies who were throwing down mattresses and blankets for the wounded.*

In spite of everything, Nora, Fatima, and Yamina did not forget my birthday. With their arms weighed down by almond cakes dripping with honey (my favorite cakes) and by roses plucked in the abandoned gardens, tonight they came to help us prepare the things that we are going to take with us. Very few things really. I'm allowed only one suitcase. We spent hours bringing up our childhood, our hearts heavy at the idea that these might be the last moments that we would spend together. Still, we're not going very far, to the other end of the rue de Lyon, to the Ruisseau, into the apartment of an Arab family threatened by the OAS. The place where I am going to live matters little! I aspire to only one thing: to get back together with Jean-Paul, and for that, I would go to the end of the Earth if necessary. I don't feel any grief at the idea of leaving our house to serve as a token of exchange, since it is about saving human lives. If only that had been decided earlier! We could have moved into Jean-Paul's house, since it is now empty! I would have then searched for the traces of his presence,"

Marie's story stops there. On a comma. I don't know where or how her path took her. Nor what she did later when the time came to relearn how to live. I would give my whole life for the same love song to resound a few instants within me. Loud enough to cover the booming of gunfire, the din of explosions, the screams, and curses. Loud enough to help me bear what awaits me.

Tonight, my aunts came to help my mother prepare the wedding cakes. Almond cakes dripping with honey. The ones Marie liked. I also will leave the house I was born in. For a new life. But I will take the notebook with me.

NOWHYBECAUSE

"So, can I . . . ?"
"No!"
"Why?"
"Because . . ."
"Because why?"
"Because that's how it is."

Variation:
"Because you can't."
"Why?"
"Because."

Because. Period. Silence.

Behind or in front of the "because" is a chasm. Or a moun-tain crowned by sharp spikes. Or a wall. So I hit against it, I dig in. I come up against this insurmountable border to which all of my questions, all of my appeals, inevitably lead me.

Every night, the moment I close my eyes, all of the letters in NOWHYBECAUSE hold hands, stretch out, scramble, elongate immeasurably, and form a chain while I run from one to the other, attempting to pass under the bar of the *A* or to jump between the two upside down legs of the *U*.[*] But they end up weaving an intricate net with such intractable threads in which I get miserably tangled.

Useless to insist, to try to understand, to jitter, to sulk, to cry, to show some revolt. Other arguments are then put into

[*] Bey's character spells out *"parce que,"* French for "because." As there is an *a, u,* and *e* in "because," I retain the child's wordplay. — *Trans.*

the works without delay. More striking, a more violent rain of punches than the period* that walls up all the exits.

Because: subordinating conjunction. Followed, under normal circumstances, by a phrase that books and teachers call: causal subordinate clause. With a verb in the indicative.

Subordinate, yes, that's it! But in our family, the causes are so indisputable that the clauses are deleted, straightaway. We only function through ellipses.

There are other causal expressions. A little syntax course. Let's enumerate:

"given that"

"the fact that"

"since"—this word is written in stone—obvious, irrefutable cause.

"seeing as"

Those, I will hear later. Sometimes with clauses that will complete the more . . . irrevocable aspect. Grammatically correct.

Concrete examples, sentences to complete, according to social, moral, and cultural realities:

"Given that you are a girl . . ."

"The fact that you're not married yet . . ."

"Seeing as he is a good catch . . ."

Let's go back to childhood.

"So, can I go play downstairs with my girlfriend?"

"No!"

"Why?"

"Because."

(Pointing to my brother) "Why him and not me?"

"Because. You can't. That's how it is."

* *"Point"* ("period") sounds similar to *"poing"* ("fist") in French, so an auditory wordplay.—*Trans.*

A few hours or a few years later.

"I'm invited to . . .'s birthday party."

"No."

"Why? All my . . ."

"No."

"But . . ."

"Quiet! Go put the dishes away!" Or (coordinating conjunction expressing choice) "go get your little brother to be quiet."

Months after. Or before.

Let's go! Be daring! Let's carefully prepare our arguments! Face the fire. With sweaty palms, heart pounding. I throw myself in:

"You know Maya, you know the one . . . yes, you know her mother, the one who lives next door to where we go buy . . ."

"Yes, so what?"

"Our math problems are due the day after tomorrow."

". . ."

"Her mother would like us to . . ."

"What?"

"us to work together."

"Where?"

"At her house."

"Why not here?"

"Because . . ."

Hold on! Role reversal. I'm the one who has to give the explanations? Should I talk at this minute about her big brother, amazing at math, who could help us? Because it's true, that was the offer her mother made. A prudence dictated by sudden clairvoyance made me hesitate. But the lie slips, comes out of me, almost without my knowledge. With a spontaneity that stuns even me.

"Her father explains the math lessons to her and helps her with the problems."

"Oh, really?"

Long silence, full of computations, calculations, approval.

"I will ask your brother to go with you and to come get you at six."

Phew! I got a normally constructed sentence, grammatically speaking, even and above all bearing a masculine element, which, as each one of us knows, trumps all.

So, it's enough to stretch the truth to make a chink. To weaken the wall.

And there! That's how we can move forward. With a muffled step, coated in lies. The route before us is strewn with direction signs outlined in red: road closed.

Walks and loitering prohibited. Don't go past this point. Dead end. Mandatory detour. You have to go the other way around.

I'm starting to understand. Yet the problem remains unsolved for a long time. That brings up numerous hypotheses. If I can't go out freely, it's because I'm too little to walk alone in the courtyard or in the street. Or that it's too warm, too cold, too dark outside, or that I have something else quite a bit more important to do—did you do your homework, clean your room, pick up your stuff lying all over the place, set or clear the table, dry the dishes, fold the laundry, wash your underwear—or the door is locked and the keys are lost, or behind the door a wolf is hiding, or a dog baring his enormous fangs, or a man all in black with a big knife . . . yes, that's it, they're scared for me. The idea reassures me. I am so precious. They want to protect me, get me out of the innumerable dangers that lie in wait for me, lurking outside. But . . . am I more precious than my brother? He goes out. He doesn't even need to ask questions, to ask permission. The doors are wide open in front of him. Or rather he opens them himself. So, what would they have to be afraid of? Maybe—and the question, vague at first, then more and more precise, slides into, rings in my ears—maybe they are afraid of me? That the dangers could come from me? That all of these desires, these impulses, this need for light and space . . .

I will learn, as the years go by, to distinguish, according to the intonation, the circumstances, the facial expressions, the repressive NOWHYBECAUSES from the protective NOWHYBE-CAUSES, rarer but every bit as definitive.

Even further still. Become a master at the art of getting around hurdles.

"You know, the teacher that was out last week . . ."

"He wants to make up his class time. Every Monday afternoon! The only day when . . ."

" . . ."

"I really don't want to . . . but it's mandatory. Do you realize, three hours of math on a Monday afternoon!"

Turns and detours.

That's the way that the NOWHYBECAUSES broke down and the way I became a specialist at hiding. Getting around.

Proven recipes. To distort. To ferret out. To trick. Maneuver to bring him or her, the one you are facing, exactly where you want them. But within the back of your throat a more and more profound disgust with yourself.

Small samples:

"Tomorrow, I can't be home at five."

"Why?"

"Because we got behind in filing. The boss decided to keep us after the offices close."

All that to go chase dreams, just for fun. To go shopping. Pretty simple. To steal a few minutes of probation through lies. With fear in the pit of your stomach.

Carefully monitored parole. Instruction: sweep away the words revolt, insubordination, expression, affirmation, dreams, ideal, make a little package wrapped in newspaper or from pages out of books, still not being able to resolve to put them in the garbage can. Leave them in the corner of the bedroom, under the bed or in a drawer, you never know. Open once in a while, inhale, as we open windows to sea breezes, and handle with precaution. Never in front of others.

And when the time comes for true confrontation, already broken off the art of argumentation, or when broken by years of weaseling, I try to bypass. But how do you go beyond silence? No more answers to questions . . . and then, no more questions.

And the rage which we no longer know how to express

comes to die at our feet, in big melting pots, before even having the time to take shape.

The wall is there, in front of a person, stiff, dense, of an insurmountable height and the chasms are darker, deeper, they crawl with words that we let fall there day after day, that at times hang on and crawl along the walls to try to come back to the surface but that are discouraged by the steep ones.

All that remains is the illusion of speech. That says everything, except the essential.

Later, even later, holding onto life in spite of everything, to the children who will be born, who are going to be, who are here . . . how do we then answer her when she asks with this light of innocence dancing in her eyes, that light that we no longer have within us:

"So, Mom, can I . . . ?"

NIGHT AND SILENCE

Night and silence weigh on my eyelids and on my sore fore-head. I can't even move. Still tonight I am not afraid, I am not hungry, I am not cold. I want to simply sleep, but I can't man-age to. Too much night, too much silence. I am lying in a bed. I can turn on the light if I want. There is a little lamp, next to me.

I can't manage to sleep. It is this slight quiver that's keeping me awake. I've been feeling a wiggling in my stomach for a little while. Yes, a slight barely perceptible rub, a ripple, as if a fish, locked in a grotto at the very bottom of the sea, inaccessible, was bumping against the walls of a dark prison. Right there, it's beginning again. It is a strange sensation. Something is moving, slipping, rubbing me within, from within. Something alive. A furtive, damp shift, a foreign body inside me.

It's the first time I feel this presence. But I already knew. Ever since the blood stopped, over there, I was afraid that it was hap-pening to me. At the beginning, I thought it was because I was hurting too much, inside me, after what they did to me. But I know that these things happen when we *meet a man*. From the numerous times I heard my mother, of hearing her say without even being shocked or complaining, no never, I still hear her saying in a weary voice, without speaking to anyone, this sen-tence whose meaning I did not at first understand: *I'm carrying a burden again*, and she used to add: one more. That's how she used to say it. How many times have I heard these words, I really had to try to understand what she wanted to say. And then I saw her body, regularly transformed. She was not fat like khalti Aïcha, so you could see it right away. And when we went to the hammam in the city, she could no longer hide her stomach in her wide dresses, her breasts with the almost black and very damaged nipples. My mother was still beautiful.

My breasts are swollen; hurt me at the least movement. I thought at first that it was because of the punches, or . . . because of their hands . . . or even of fatigue, of the buckets that I carried all day, my exhausted arms, but I understood that that's what it was. And I didn't tell anyone. I was too scared.

Back there, it was Kheïra who first noticed. One morning, while I was trying to wash myself at the edge of the wadi, she saw my breasts. A simple look was enough for her. She said passing in front of me, "Careful! It's going to be your turn now." Then she looked away very quickly, before they surprised us talking. We weren't allowed. They watched over us all the time. A little later, passing in front of me again, she threw me a bloody rag without saying anything to me. I picked it up right away. It didn't take me very much time to understand. I wore it between my legs for several days and, believing me impure, nobody approached me. They stopped interrogating me. Maybe that's what saved me. They could have done to me what they did to Lila. They took her as soon as they realized she was pregnant. Their wives informed them. Snitches! Always spying on us, giving us orders, denouncing us, forcing us to obey. One day they kicked Lila in the stomach in front of us. And in the evening, since she could not get up, they dragged her away. Ever since, we haven't seen her.

Yes, I'm here thanks to Kheïra. What has become of her? Is she still over there? May God forgive me, I have not thought of her again since the day I ran away. They must have killed her now, because of me maybe. Or then . . . none among us could hold up over there for such a long time. She was brought to the camp a few weeks after me. I remember her look, afterward . . . They all, they all took her, in the same night. All, one after the other. She cried out a little, at the beginning, like all of us. And she ended up shutting up. Like us. I still remember the blonde Fadela who used to say, "They have something to keep them busy tonight. We will be able to sleep." That's how she used to say it! Without the least emotion. Hard and cold. She'd been like that since her arrival, or before, I don't know. Even with us. One would have said that nothing could reach her. Those were her last words, by the way. She too ended up escaping them that same night. In silence. God! Their fury when they discovered in the wee hours of the morning her body that was hanging barely a few centimeters above the ground! She had tied several knots in her scarf, and they had trouble untying her from the tree. They took their revenge on her body, but they could no longer do anything to her, she was only a corpse. Afterward, they turned on us.

She escaped from them. I wanted to, too. The following nights, I dreamed that she was coming to me, clothed in white, that she was holding out her hand, trying to pull me along. She was telling me in a very soft voice, "Follow me . . . follow me, I know the way, you only have to follow me." And I was trying to get up in my dream, and I couldn't. I was heavy. My feet were attached to stakes solidly planted in the ground. I would have liked it if she untied me, but I couldn't say anything to her. I had no voice, I couldn't even signal to her. Then she was going away, turning around one last time and disappearing, drowned in cloud.

They've put me in a room alone. Maybe that's why I can't sleep. Because I'm alone and everything is quiet. I'm not used to it. I have never slept alone in a room. At home, we used to sleep all together, in the same room. We had only two rooms and my father and my mother were in the other with the newborn's cradle. In the family room, we laid out the mattresses on the ground: my brothers on one side, my little sisters and I on the other. In the winter, we all huddled together under a big blanket. And we were warm. And tonight, I'm alone. I'm alone forever. I have no more brothers. No more sisters, nothing left of my own. My father, my mother, my brothers, all of them, they are all dead. I know it. I heard them scream while they dragged me outside. Why didn't they kill me with them? Why, my God? I no longer have anyone. There is . . . there is only that thing in my stomach. No, I should no longer be thinking about that. I have to try to find sleep. Last night, they made me swallow tablets. Three little white pills. I slept. I felt myself slip very quickly into sleep. I had no dreams. And it had been daylight for a long time when I opened my eyes. The sun lit up the whole room. And there was a woman seated on a chair, next to me. She was looking at me. She waited a minute and asked me if I wanted to get up. There was also a tray with a cup and some bread on the table. She held it out to me. I closed my eyes. I felt like I was in cotton. Everything was blurry, soft. Probably because of the pills. She asked me if I wanted to get up. If I wanted to talk. I couldn't even answer her. She stayed there looking at me for a long time, without moving. In silence. I barely heard her breathe. I had my eyes closed, but I felt her presence. She wasn't a woman from our town. She had short hair. A bare head. She looked like those women that you see on television. Or the ones who live in cities. I know that there are women who come and go in the cities without a veil, without a djellaba. Before, there were some who came to us, in the douar, just like that. Bareheaded. As children, we followed them. Astonished. It seemed very funny to us that they would dress like men, that they would walk like them, by their side. That they would sit outside, without being bothered by men's looks. Foreigners. But some of them came inside the houses and spoke with us. In the same language. We had a hard time believing that they were Algerians like us. In our town, women did not go out without veiling their head. And they never sat with the men. My mother told me that in cities, certain women leave their homes every day to work with men in offices. There are even some who drive cars. We see them on television. Not where we're from.

This woman has a soft voice, very soft. She talked to me. She said the same thing as the others, "You're here, with us. You don't have to be afraid. It's over. You can open your eyes, no one will hurt you anymore." Then she was quiet, for a long time. She called me, from time to time. She pronounced my name, several times. But I kept my eyes closed. I wanted to hear her again. I liked her voice. I was warm under the blanket. I didn't want to move. When I felt her hand on my hair, that's when I cried out. I don't want people touching me. Never again. After a while, she got up and told me again, "Don't be afraid. I don't want to hurt you. I will come back to see you." And then she went out. She closed the door and I heard her

speaking with someone in the hallway. I didn't understand
what she said. A bit later, other people came. Men and women.
They stayed standing around the bed. They, also, wanted to
talk to me. But I hid my face and I turned toward the wall. I
was too ashamed. The room was crowded. They were talking
about me among themselves. I wasn't even trying to understand
what they were saying. Besides, many were speaking French. As
for me, at school, I didn't have time to learn French. My father
made me leave school at nine to help my mother. When they all
left, I opened my eyes. Another woman came in. She brought
me a tray. She set it on the table. *She* didn't speak to me. She left
again right away. I looked. There was a piece of meat and some
potatoes on a plate. It was for me. I ate because I was really
hungry. That's all. And then, it was night again. I couldn't get
up. Even when they left me alone:

I can't sleep. *Sleep has flown from me.* There are too many
things buzzing in my head. If I keep thinking about all that, I
will never be able to sleep. I should have asked them to give
me pills again. There is too much silence. The walls are thick. I
don't even know where I am. The soldiers told me: "We're going to take you to a center in Algiers." It's my first time coming
to Algiers. But when I was in the car, I didn't see anything. I
had my head down. Because of the men who were sitting next
to me. And when the car stopped, they made me go in here right
away. I sat down. I did not know what to do. The soldiers interrogated me again. I answered all their questions. They wanted
to know everything. I said what I knew. Then people came in
with cameras. They asked me my name, my age. They made me
repeat my age. My head hurt very badly. My eyes hurt from
the lights that flickered. I would have liked to be somewhere
else. I was so ashamed. They said, "*Meskina, meskina,* poor
thing . . ." That's all I was able to understand. And that made
me want to cry. To scream.

It's been a long time since I've cried. I howled, I cried, wept,
begged, prayed, the night that they came into our house. Especially the moment when they found my little brother, Ali. My
mother had had the time to hide him in a corner of the room,
under a small table. But he cried out. *She* had understood right

away. If he hadn't cried out, maybe they wouldn't have found him. When I saw one of them turn around and go to look for him, I threw myself on him. I wanted to keep him from being beaten or hit. I was saying to him, "He is very small, let him go, let him go, he didn't do anything, he doesn't know anything!" But he pushed me back. He gave me a kick in the ribs. I didn't feel anything. I kept on holding his leg to keep him from coming up to Ali. I dragged myself on the ground. And another caught Ali. He didn't even put up a fight. He caught his foot, and he held him like that, upside down. Then he left. I heard him scream. Only once. He was two. He was starting to talk. He said my name first. *Dida.* He couldn't pronounce it properly.

I wonder why they kill children, the littlest ones. One day I put the question to one of the women, at the camp where we were. She laughed. She told me, "When there are cockroaches in the house, if we want to get rid of them, you have to kill them all! Exterminate them! If not, they proliferate again, didn't you know?" and she kept on laughing. I didn't really understand. But another time, I heard them say that it was to save them, to save the still-innocent children, to keep them from becoming unbelievers, like their parents. It was their leader, the Emir, who was explaining it. And they were all listening.

I miss Ali. At night, he could only sleep if I took him and hugged him tightly in my arms. I was thirteen when he was born. I was already grown up. He laid his head on my chest and didn't move anymore. I feel like there is an emptiness, there where he was. There. My little one! *My* little one! He was entirely mine. My mother never had to take care of him. I even tried to breastfeed him, once. He sucked for a while and that made me feel weird. My whole body trembled. The whole time I was there, I tried not to think about him. It hurt too much. I would like them to let me go to his grave, if he has one. If I go back to the douar one day. I saw that they had set several houses on fire, ours too, before they took us. There must be nothing left.

Over there, in the camp, I used to fall asleep right away. As soon as they were done with me. I had to wait until they were willing to let me go back to my corner, at the back of the grotto. It could last a long time. But even so I had a few hours of rest every night. I slept anywhere, no matter how. I only had to close my eyes and I used to crash very quickly. I didn't used to sleep much, but I felt like I was diving into an abyss, and everything would disappear for a few hours. Until they came to wake us up, at the first gleams of daylight. It's because the days were tiring. We didn't have time to think back, to remember. Maybe it was better that way. We weren't allowed to stop even for a minute. Between the water buckets, the loads of laundry, the meals to prepare for everyone, there was a lot to do.

Oh! God! If I could erase all that! How do you make yourself not think about it? No, I don't want to forget, it's impossible. Only to stop thinking about it. But how to wipe everything out with this thing quivering in my stomach? If I could empty my head! Only for a few minutes. The time it takes for sleep to overtake me, to engulf me. Maybe by praying or by reciting the *Chahada* . . . but I already tried . . . and that's even harder. As soon as I pronounce the first words, I feel like they are here. I hear their voices. God, forgive me! I can no longer say those words. That's how they used to start everything they did: *"In God's name."* Without stopping. Before drinking. Before eating. Before punishing us. Before killing. They invoked God at every moment. When they came to our door, they were screaming: *"Allah ou akbar!"* That is how we found out right away who they were. And my father opened the door for them, without mistrust. He thought his son Djamel was with them. Since he had gone up to join the maquis, we didn't even know if he was still alive. We couldn't even think for one minute that they had killed him. Not them! Later, they told me what had happened.

But what's the use of going back over it now? Nothing can ever be like before. I want so much to sleep . . . to sleep.

When she comes back, I will have to talk to her.

I didn't sin, she has to know that.

If my father and brothers were still alive, they would have killed me. So as not to have to face the dishonor. And I would have let them do it. What's going to become of me now? I

can never go back to our douar. Even the people I'm clos-
est to would not want anything to do with me. Who would
want to take me in? To feed me? But what remains of our
douar? I should have cried out, not put up with it. I should have
pushed them to kill me. I want to die. Who is going to want
to have anything to do with me now? I dishonored the family.

I don't want anything to do with this being that moves inside me. I don't want to give life to a being that could look like
them. I want them to take this thing out of me that is going to
grow in my stomach if I don't stop it. Let them eliminate it, or
eliminate me. That's the best thing to do. They can't make me
bring it into the world! They can't make me take it in my arms,
to feed it with my milk, to let it grow up to hate, kill, or get
itself killed.

When this woman comes back to see me, I will speak to her.
Maybe I could explain to her. She will certainly understand.
She is a woman who must have children. When she smiles,
her eyes also smile, like my mother's. Maybe she has a daughter my age, or older. And even if she has no children, she's a
woman. Only women can understand these things. She seems
so sweet. She will listen to me. She will talk to the doctor herself. I didn't say anything to that doctor who came to examine
me. He's a man. He was satisfied when he lit a little light that
he pointed at my eyes. He blinded me. Then he listened to my
heart with an instrument that was so cold that I shivered. I
didn't want to take off my clothes. He only asked me if I ate
over there. It's true, I'm very skinny. But I've always been that
way. He said "over there" to describe the camp in the forest.
He also asked me how long I had been with them. I didn't know
how to answer him. We didn't used to count the days. We
dreaded the dark too much. We would have liked to will the
sun never to set. I must have spent hundreds of nights over
there. Or more. I don't know. The night when they came to the
douar to avenge my brother's betrayal, it was very hot. It was
summer. And now, it's winter. It is very cold. It was very cold
over there. How much time? Why is that important? When we
know we're in hell, time doesn't exist. We only wait for true
death. The end of everything. Deliverance.

That's it. Now they know. They know I'm carrying within me the fruit of a sin that I didn't commit.

I didn't want to take off my clothes in front of the woman. However she went with me when they took me to the shower. She stayed with me. She brought me new clothes and told me I couldn't wear them if I didn't wash. I was ashamed. Ashamed of my filth. Ashamed of the lice that were crawling in my hair. Of the blue marks that I have all over my body. While running in the forest I fell on stones. I scratched myself on the underbrush. My legs are covered in crusts of blood. She gave me some soap, a towel and plastic flip-flops. I stayed in the shower's warm water for a long, long time. I would have liked everything to go away with the water, dirty, so dirty when it slipped over my body. I rubbed myself so hard that I scraped my skin off. But that didn't do anything. I felt just as dirty inside. The scabbed wounds reopened and began to bleed again. The water was red. I had a hard time putting on the underwear she had prepared. Not because of that. Because of her look. She looked at my breasts. I surprised her look. Her astonishment. She averted her eyes very quickly. Without saying anything. Then she went toward the window. She stayed there standing a long while. When she turned around, her eyes were full of tears. She asked me my age. I said fifteen. But she must have known that. I had already told the soldiers who had interrogated me. She wanted to be sure, I think. Then I said I wanted scissors. She jumped. I pointed to my hair.

She understood that I was carrying a being in my stomach. I saw it in her eyes. And before leaving the center, she certainly said it to the others, to the ones who are behind the door. And now everybody knows. The doctor came by to see me a little bit later. He looked flustered. He said they were going to take me to a hospital for some tests. Why don't they leave me be? I don't need anything.

The sun disappeared. The sky is red. It is winter. Night falls very quickly. It's already very dark in the room. From my bed, I can see leaves. The window is low. It looks out over a garden, at the back of the building. Nobody walks in the paths of this garden.

The other woman is going to come. She is going to bring me my meal. She never speaks. She doesn't even look at me. From now on, I am not going to eat anymore. That way, this thing in my stomach will not be able to feed itself. And if God has pity on me, he will understand, will help me die to retrieve my purity.

Evil will grow within me. I feel it. It is taking shape. It could have their eyes, full of madness. Their hands, so hard, so dirty. Their desire to make other beings suffer. Yes, it could be like them. I feel it. It moves. It awaits its time. They beat me. They dishonored me. They spread their cursed semen in me so that I could neither forget, nor relive again. Every night the devil hung onto their beard. Marked forever. What is a dishonored girl worth? Who will ever understand? I have to foil their plans.

Now night has fallen. There are still the sounds of steps in the hallway. Maybe there are other girls here. Girls who suffered the same fate as me. I don't want to see them. I don't want to see anyone. Silence is going to cover everything over again soon. I shouldn't be afraid. God is protecting me. He alone knows that I am innocent. And if He hears me, if He hears my prayer, He will soon deliver me from this torture. I will go find my loved ones again. Especially Ali. He was only a child. I carried him on my back when he didn't know how to walk. I fed him. I gave him all the love that my mother couldn't give him. Because she didn't have time. Because she was too tired to care for him. I was the first girl. I did everything to support her. She often used to say that she didn't know what she would do when the time came for me to leave the house. She wanted me to get married too. To have children. I know how to take care of children very well. How to change them, how to wash them, how to rock them, how to sing them songs. What joy to carry a child in your arms, to see him smile when we talk to him! My mother often tried to *let the being fall out of her stomach*. She took bitter concoctions that khalti Aïcha prepared for her. She carried very heavy weights for hours. She even tried to jump

from the top of the small wall that surrounded the little bit of
garden that she grew. But nothing did it. Over there, I carried
water buckets. By tens. Every day. And one night, while they
were conducting raids, I ran. All night long. I fell. I knocked
myself against big rocks. I crawled. I got back up. And I ran a
long time. I thought about nothing. I wanted to go to the end
of the world. Or to die. But I am still here this evening. And I
am alive. Death didn't want anything to do with me. I have to
expiate. But I am innocent. I should have, yes, I should have
done the same thing as Fadela. *She,* at least, is delivered from
everything today. Nothing else can reach her. I have to pray.
That I implore God to deliver me too. I have to put myself in
His hands. Men can't do anything for me. And above all, I
don't want their pity.

Her name is Aïcha. Like my aunt. She came back a little
while ago, in the early afternoon. She brought me scissors, perfume, and a comb. She talked to me. She showed me a picture of her two daughters. Twins. They're my age. I was right.
One of them, the brown-haired one, even looks a little bit like
me. That's what she told me. They are both very beautiful.
They have happiness and love all around them. You can see it.
I asked her if the photo had been taken in their room. Because
they were sitting behind a big desk and had books open in front
of them. I thought it was a school. The wall behind them was
covered with color portraits, huge ones. She laughed when I
asked her if they were her family members' portraits. I don't
yet understand why she comes every day, what she expects of
me. But I don't dare ask her. All she does is sit near me, look
at me, try to make me talk. I told her the story about my brother
Djamel, because I didn't want to talk about myself. I talked for
a long time. She asked me no questions. She was content to nod
her head and listen to me. From time to time, she got up and
went to the window. I didn't see her face, but I knew it was
because she didn't want to show me that this was difficult for
her. I told her everything. They told me his story in the camp. I
told her that he had been with them, in the maquis, for several
months. That he had tried to run away with a girl that they had

taken to the camp before me. That he wanted to save her because he loved her. I told her how they were denounced, caught again, tortured for hours before they died together. She listened and sometimes took her head in her hands, as if she were hurting. Then, I quieted. I think that was adequate.

She was still with me when the doctor came to tell me that they were going to keep me at the center until the child's birth. What child? And then? That's all I said. It came out of me like a scream. He raised his eyebrows to signal that he didn't know. That was his answer. That's when I looked him straight in the eyes and I told him that I'd rather die than wait until then. He turned his head away, as if he couldn't stand my eyes on him, or as if he didn't want to listen to me. Without adding anything more, he put away his files and went out. He'd done his job.

When we were alone again, she sat on the bed, very close to me. She took my hand. I didn't pull it back. She asked me questions about my life in the douar, before. About what I liked. I couldn't utter Ali's name. I told her the story about my tree, the one that my grandmother planted on the day of my birth. It's a fig tree that grew up at the same time as me. It had only been bearing fruit for three summers. And ever since, I looked impatiently under each leaf, waiting for the first sign of the figs. I plucked them myself. Sometimes, I filled little wicker baskets that I lined with beautiful green leaves and, with my little brothers, I went to sell them to the people driving by on the highway. The money I earned, I gave to my mother. She hid it for me. For later. While talking, the coolness and taste of the red flesh packed with sugar was coming back to me, the crunch of seeds in my mouth and, for a few instants, I forgot where I was. I felt like I was going back to the light of summer afternoons that I spent dreaming or sleeping under my tree, near the house. It must still be standing, over there. It must have given beautiful figs this year. I just hope that they did not let them rot.

She listened to me with a smile, as if she too had the taste of figs in her mouth. Then she told me she had to leave. That she would come back, and that I had to think of all those things, of everything that continues. Only about that.

She left. She took a few steps in the hallway, then she came back. She had forgotten to give me the scarf that was in her bag. A big white scarf, edged with little shiny pearls, like drops of water.

Near the end of the day, I got up. I opened the window. When the other woman came in with her tray, I asked her if I could go outside to take a little walk in the garden.

She pointed her finger to show me it was very dark, and she told me that the door that you could glimpse from the window led down into a ravine. She said no one went to that side. It was too dangerous. Especially at night. I didn't understand right away why she was telling me that. I just wanted to take a walk. I didn't want to run away. But she then added that in olden days a wild woman used to live there, whose story no one knew. That certain people said they could hear her howling at night, at the very bottom of the ravine, and that she appeared clothed in white when they announced a woman's death.

Ever since, no one has come into the room. Night has now fallen over the garden. Everything is still quiet.

Algiers, January 2000

WOMAN'S HAND AT THE WINDOW

Sunday, 7:00 a.m.

Her hand is laid on the window sill, between two bars. A very white, almost opalescent hand, with very thin fingers, with clipped nails, with blue veins. A woman's hand reposing in sleep's surrender. Her palm is turned upward, as if in a gesture of imploration.

He only sees this still yet supple hand, as if detached from a body lurking in the shadows, a presence that he does not even think about picturing.

The window is high enough. The blinds are pulled down. Only one window is open, masked by a white curtain that rises from time to time with the breath of a slight breeze or the sleeping woman's sigh.

Almost in spite of himself, he slows his step. In enough time to perhaps surprise a movement.

He is now so close to her hand that he could almost touch it, simply by raising his arm.

The street is deserted. In the pale light that is falling from the still-lit streetlights, only the noise of his steps comes to trouble the calm of the still-misty dawn hours.

A few meters farther on, he cannot keep himself from turning around as if to assure himself of the reality of what he has just seen. Her hand is still laid on the window sill, immobile. From there, were it not for its translucent appearance, you could take it for a branch fallen from a tree and left there out of carelessness. He abruptly remembers that as a very small boy, he often had fun playing a game where plants or parts of

Written in homage to the victims recovered or missing, to the children, women, and men who were victims of the civil authorities' mismanagement and of the flood on November 10, 2001, in Algiers. —*Author* plants or vegetable matter were paired with parts of the human body. He shivers abruptly. The air is cool at this time of the morning. He turns up his jacket collar, buries his hands in his pockets, and walks away with long strides.

Sunday Evening

Before reaching the corner of the small street, he remembers this hand negligently posed on the window sill. A quickly forgotten sight in the agitation that held sway in the ward, and that now is imposed on him, with such exactness that he at first believes it to be taken out of one of his dreams. He again sees the stream-lined fingers, the back of her hand with small apparent veins running through it. The squared end of her thumb set slightly apart from her other fingers. His imagination even helps him to go a little bit further. He imagines her wrist, stiff joints, marked with a slight bulge at the base. A woman's hand slipped into the opening of a half-closed window. That would make for the beginning of a beautiful story. An unusual little tale full of mystery. Hand of an unknown odalisque, hand of a captive, hand offered in a gesture of surrender to the first passerby of the day.

The sun stands still in a last blaze. While he moves forward, his shadow stretches out immeasurably on the sidewalk. Three young children jostle each other running after a traumatized cat that sneaks through the gates around the neighboring house's garden. Miffed, they put their heads together before turning back. They utter words he does not understand. He arrives in front of the house, throws a glance at the window. It is closed. The shutters are lowered. The cat is now perched on the ledge, behind the bars, out of reach. All of the light of the ending day seems focused in the slant of the wide eyes fixed on him for a long time after he looked away.

Monday Morning

He does not remember his dream, but an unusual malaise fills him. He only retained scrambled fragments, confused and disparate images, pieces of a puzzle that he cannot put together. Thirsty, as if out of breath, he has woken up several times in the night. He will be late this morning. It matters little, his operation schedule is not busy this morning. A gall bladder and a hydatid cyst in a liver. Routine. As long as a colleague, seeing that he has not yet arrived, does not get the idea to occupy the operating room before him. He wants to have done with it very quickly to go home and rest. At least that is what he hopes, still knowing very well that he will not return before nightfall, as always. As he turns the key in the lock, he hears the telephone ringing. He hesitates a moment and then finishes closing the door behind him. If it is the hospital, he will be there in twenty minutes. He quickens his step. Nothing like a good walk before starting work. With the usual mental stimulation. Focusing on the present moment, the still-soft colors of the morning, the freshness of the air, the noise of the wind in the trees—and only on that. It is the only way for him to empty his mind of what is weighing it down before facing the multiple daily concerns in the ward, other people's pain, the show of physical decline, the complaints, the faces of patients and of those close to them deformed by anxious worry that sends him back to his own suffering.

Monday's commute. In the direction of the naval complex of El Kettani. There, the clatter of waves smashing against the cliffs totally absorbs him. For some time, he avoids always taking the same route. That is part of his strategy to fight against becoming stuck, routine, and above all despair. But . . . he abruptly begins to think that taking the same path each Monday is also to confront his rituals! Internally cursing his inability to let himself be carried away by the unexpected in life, he veers off.

At the moment when he arrives in front of the house, he remembers his dream. A dream of regression. As a very small boy in his mother's arms, he used to let himself indulge in a sentiment of total beatitude before noticing, when he looked up, that this woman who was hugging him so tightly against her was not his mother. However, before he could identify the woman who was holding him in her arms, she had her hand over his eyes. The contact of this soft skin, the gentleness of her fingers laid over his face, the so specific and so penetrating perfume that imbued her hand and her clothes against which he had placed his cheek had thrown him into such a severe confusion that he had freed himself very quickly, had opened a window, and in one leap found himself naked on the side-walk, again become a man across from a pack of children who watched him while taunting him. It seems that he can still hear this taunting. It's the first time in a long while that he has re-created a dream with so much precision.

The window is half-open. The curtains are pulled, but the panes only send back the shaky reflection of an exuberant bou-gainvillea. There is no one in the street. Pushed by an irresist-ible impulse, he leans forward, standing slightly on his tiptoes. Through the half-open window, he discerns, at the end of a dark space, a pool of light, a gate open on a garden or a court-yard, and, right in the middle of his field of vision, a trough, entirely covered with small white tiles decorated with blue and gold arabesques. And, playing in the water that overflows and trickles into a circular basin right underneath, he glimpses only a hand, which rises and lets itself fall back in a steady move-ment, full of grace and nonchalance.

Wednesday Evening

For two days, he has taken an increasing number of detours to avoid passing through the small street, and walking alongside the house. For two days, he has kept thinking about this half-glimpsed scene, he has been hearing the water's murmur, he has even been feeling its freshness on his hands. The image is frozen in his brain. The gesture tirelessly repeats, to the point where it obsesses him. At the moment when he seizes his scalpel, raises his hand to make an incision. He has a bizarre feeling: that it is not his hand which falls back. Its stroke is light as a feather, another caressing hand that clutches and guides his with a poignant softness. And for a few minutes, his hands trembling, he has to make an effort to focus on the body lying in front of him, to pull himself together to go through with the gestures that he has repeated a thousand times.

He just finished his rounds in the ward. He lingered next to this child operated on the day before; and before the eyes of the astonished interns, he could not keep himself from caressing his forehead, while talking to him. Usually, he doesn't let himself indulge in compassion. Since he has to be so close to death, he had to learn very quickly how to protect himself. Even more so now. But little Farid's eyes were fixed on him with so much trust that he felt something melt within him, a sensation come from very far back. He examined the incision that ran across his stomach, happily surprised by its clean appearance, with no puss or blister. It will heal rapidly.

As he leaves the hospital, he decides to postpone the moment when he goes home. For the first time in long weeks, he does not want to be alone. He mingles a minute in the crowd of people out for an evening stroll on the boulevard Front de mer. The air is filled with sea smells, and the day seems to linger in shimmering quivers on the water's surface. October is drawing to a close, and summer has not taken its leave. He lets himself be carried away by this animated stream without resisting, which flows very slowly. He recognizes certain faces, answers greetings. The rows of streetlights come on one after the other, and the streets empty bit by bit as he returns home, in the dwindling hum of the day.

Thursday Evening

That could be the detail in a painting. Sketched by hand. Studies in charcoal. He scrutinizes, examines with a magnifying glass, studies. Woman's Hand at the Window. The Orientalists above all. Certainly because of the small white tiles decorated with arabesques. Delacroix. Fromentin. Gérôme. Then turns to the sketches. He again immerses himself in the art books long forgotten on his living room bookshelf. An old passion that he rediscovers, astonishingly intact. Movements grasped, frozen flights in a painter's gaze. Then he finds this sculpture by Rodin. He takes a long look at this *Hand of God*. This man and woman's embracing in an enormous hand, half-closed over its palm. Trap or destiny? Hardness, eternity of bronze, fragility of this half-seen hand, which has been haunting his dreams for a few days. Outstretched beseeching hand, closed hand, clenched fists, idle hands, joined hands, callous, deformed, gaunt hands. He again takes up his anatomy textbooks. Carpals and metacarpals, tendons, reticulanum, extensors. Here, he feels more at ease.

He cannot manage to imagine the body and face of this woman, whose existence he sometimes doubts. And then above all, he knows that he will not have the strength to go through with this risky exercise. He registers only one face.

This evening, before going home, he took a detour. He rapidly passed through the little barely lit street. Then he backtracked, stopped across from the house in hopes of surprising some trace of life, to see the door finally open. Not one ray of light behind the closed shutters. Still, he thought he heard children's shouts and laughter. He lit a cigarette and waited for a few minutes before leaving again.

When he returned home, he found several messages on his answering machine. Always the same words, the same requests. "You should make an effort, at least for our sake. We're here . . ." One of them is broken up by sobs and silences. He did not even have to think to recognize the voice. It is probably Sarah's sister. He pressed the button very quickly to erase everything. He does not need anyone.

Friday Morning

Day of rest. He wakes very early and cannot go back to sleep, despite his desire to stay immersed in sleep's void for as long as possible. Too much solitude, too much silence.

He sits on the edge of the bed. Always the same gestures.

He turns around, mechanically turns on the radio. The outer world abruptly engulfs him. News. He turns the dial. He does not want to know anything about other people's lives.

7:00 a.m. He looks at himself in the mirror, runs his hand over his rough chin. He will shave tomorrow, before going to work.

Still long hours trying not to uncover the memories that could reopen his wound.

Sunday Evening

To grasp her outstretched hand. To experience through touch her consistency, her reality, her softness.

Why did he think pain?

Thursday, 11:00 p.m.

He emerges brutally from a restless sleep. He is suffocating. He fell asleep in his armchair, still dressed. He dreamed that he let himself sink into muddy water without moving his arms, without being able to make the least movement.

No! Rather, without wanting to make the least movement. Photos scattered around him on the rug. He does not pick them up.

Saturday Morning

He is greeted at the ward's entrance by Farid, who was waiting for him to say good-bye and thank you. He then remembered that he had signed the discharge form earlier than expected because of the little boy's spectacular recovery. Behind the child, the mother's shining face, grasping his hand and pressing it to her lips. He steals away with a quick gesture, mutters an excuse, and locks himself in his office.

He examines the files laid on his desk; three surgeries are

scheduled today. He nods his head pensively. One of them will be particularly tricky. Very guarded prognosis. It's a last-ditch operation. And even so . . . he is not sure. Maybe he should put it off . . . let the patient go slowly.

He gets up, goes toward the window. Seated on a bench, two old women, their heads thrown back, eyes closed, seem to want to soak up the sun. All around them, dried-up yellow plants are curled in on themselves, as if to preserve themselves, waiting for better days. Above some trees with crackling foliage, the sky is an inalterable blue. He looks at the two women turned to the light for a long time, then he takes his lab coat off the hook and heads for the door.

"We will not grow old together," she said, attempting to hold his hand in a last effort. And she closed her eyes.

Sunday Evening

His mother had come while he was out. She put everything away, dusted, changed the sheets, cleaned the bathroom, and took away his dirty laundry to wash at her house. He doesn't even think about picking up the telephone, to call her to thank her. He knows that he cannot bear the worried tone that she has always assumed since the accident, and the affectionate reproaches that she will not miss the chance to say. He does not yet feel capable of answering, of finding the words to justify himself. Not yet. He writes "thank you," nothing more, on a piece of paper that he leaves prominently on the kitchen table. She will find it when she comes back tomorrow morning to drop off his ironed shirts. They are beginning to get organized.

Three months now.

Three months already.

And always this frightening emptiness in the place of his heart.

This silence that greets him every evening.

Sarah.

He hears himself utter her name for the first time out loud, as if she could hear him. He tries to find the intonation, the call, the certainty of being heard. But the name comes off in the silence, and falls back, like a stone.

Very early this morning, he went by the house again. This time the window was wide open. He even heard, or thought he heard, accompanied by an old Andalusian air, a woman's song that seemed to come from the house's center. The wind puffed the curtains out and stuck them to the bars.

When he got farther away, he jumped at the click of a window that someone was closing.

Friday, Noon

He pulls an armchair onto the balcony and settles down, book in hand.

A few white wisps dissipate in the sky, followed a few instants later by denser clouds that come rushing in and accumulate to mask the sun. Finally! Would they come bearing rain? He does not dare believe it. Yesterday morning, the whole city resounded with calls to prayer for rain. Everywhere, in all the country's mosques, they implored heaven. Rituals from another age. The temptation for the irrational becomes stronger and stronger. You would think that everything is going irremediably haywire. One must look into men's hearts for the true reasons for the drought that has been reigning for so many years throughout the country.

An abrupt gust of wind turns the pages of the book abandoned on his knees.

Saturday, 5:00 a.m.

He is pulled out of sleep by a long lament. He very quickly recognizes the howl under the bedroom's French door, a howl covered by an at first far-off, then more and more distinct, drumming. Shutters slam in the night. The claps of thunder, flashes fleetingly illuminating the room, and finally the great drumming of the rain, the same as the trampling of an innumerable herd surging into the city.

He does not fall right back to sleep.

Saturday, 8:30 a.m.

The storm isn't weakening.

He only has a few meters to go in the rain to get to the garage. It's the first time since the accident that he has taken the car out. He didn't even think about bringing an umbrella, and, in a few seconds, he is soaked.

He sits at the steering wheel, turns the key in the ignition, and is a little bit surprised by the motor's immediate reaction when it starts to purr. He turns on the windshield wipers, shifts gears. It will certainly take more time to get to the hospital than when he covers the same distance on foot. Traffic is heavy. On rainy days, everybody has the same impulse.

On the sidewalks, passersby whipped by the increasingly violent downpour move forward with difficulty. The sky, urgently called into action, redoubled its efforts. As if, in excess of exceptional generosity, or in order to no longer hear men's lamentations, it wanted to erase in one day long months of drought and dust.

He drives very slowly. At the intersection, the police are trying their best to channel the flow of numerous cars all driven by these drivers in a hurry to get to work. Water is overflowing from the culverts, the sewers that haven't been treated in early fall are certainly obstructed by the trash accumulated over months, and passersby splattered by passing cars and buses crammed with workers let irate curses flow.

At this rate, it will certainly take him over an hour to make it to the ward. He turns to the left, comes out into the little street, also crowded with vehicles that are moving awkwardly forward, bumper to bumper.

He is stopped by the house when the torrent of mud makes it beyond the street corner. A black wave, loaded down by wet trash and debris, a silent gush, so high, so powerful that it covers all the cars, and drags them away one after the other.

He doesn't see the mudflow that surges and is going to reach his car. At this exact instant, he has his eyes fixed on the windows of the house, surprised to see them open in spite of the downpour.

He only turns around at the last moment. His car is shaken so in the shock that he thinks at first that it was an accident.

Sarah's astonished face when he had bent over her after the crash . . .

He has just enough time to open the door before being swept up.

Saturday, November 10, 2001, 6:00 p.m.

How long has he been sitting in his armchair?

He is alone in his living room.

On the low table, two candles are lit. No more electricity in the neighborhood. Maybe even in the whole city.

He is sitting in the semi-darkness, his head in his hands, shivers running down his body.

He has the bitter taste of earth in his mouth and, on his skin, the smell of rot that he hasn't been able to get off in the shower.

His soiled clothes lie on the rug around him.

For long hours he has not said a word. To anyone.

He remembers nothing.

He simply remembers hanging on with all his might to a hand that was stretching toward him at the moment when he was going to be swept away.

"WHAT'S AN ARAB?"

Childhood.
I plunge my hands into formlessness. I search. Warm quick
sands. I get stuck.

Take one: a question.

The child stands. Up straight. She raises her head, protects
herself from the sun using her hand as a visor and asks:
"What's an Arab?"

I can't see the face again. I no longer know why or to whom
I asked the question. Certainly to an adult. To someone much
taller than I am because I have to lift my head. Since logically,
only adults can answer questions. Nevertheless, I don't have
the answer. I can't find it again in my memory. Maybe they
didn't answer me. Or that the answer, too evasive or too high-
brow, didn't convince me, didn't enlighten me. Adults often give
any old answer to get rid of overly curious children.
Still the word makes images jump out.
Grasp them before they are altered by present certainties.
Maybe the answer is there.

Her aunts' long, ample, one-piece dresses. On their heads,
multicolored silk scarves. Mysterious signs tattooed on their
faces, on the backs of their hands. Her grandfather's white bur-
nous and beard. Right there, precisely, a tickling. It's rough.

"What's an Arab?" was previously published in the edited short-story
collection *Une enfance outremer* (Point Seuil, 2001). —*Author*
    As with *Entendez-vous dans les montagnes . . .* , this story is autofiction
and relates to the arrest and death of Bey's father and uncles.—*Trans.*

It prickles when you kiss him. But she likes it. She is often on his lap. The movement he made when he wrapped his turban. Kilometers of white cloth.

That's it. Clichés. But maybe that's the way we will be able to move forward. Keep on going.

Gazing at her, her grandfather's eyes. Very light-colored. Green? Blue? This tenderness which dug thousands of wrinkles into his smile, deep as the riverbed.

Yes, it's right there. Still present. So present that tears come into my eyes.

Another moment stands out, escapes forgetfulness and projects itself, now there on the page. How to be sure that it has not been retold to me by my mother? Too bad. I begin.

The little girl soars to the height of knowledge. She has learned to read. Before even going to school. Simply by listening and watching her father in his class, during the night courses, and when he prepared his forms, filled his grade book, corrected students' notebooks. Each evening she sits next to him on the edge of the desk, in the light of the lamp that isolates them from the others—from the rest of the family. Then, at school, while her classmates are barely beginning to decode words, they trip over syllables, fighting with liaisons and wading through agreements, she advances at top speed, exploring territories which she already has a hard time coming back from, and discovers, as she turns pages, worlds so vast that she will never see the end of them.

She knows how to read. Sitting on her grandfather's lap, she has a book in her hands. She shows him a geography map. Here, look at this picture. It's France. Read it! It's written underneath. He laughs. Weird, he doesn't understand. He doesn't know how to read. Not her books. They didn't teach him how to do that at school when he was little. He has other books, filled with different characters. She doesn't know how to decode them. But maybe he never went to school. Vexed, disappointed not to be able to share her knowledge, the little girl frees herself from her grandfather's arms and finds refuge on her father's lap.

No, something's wrong! The ending has to be rewritten. That doesn't correspond to what I know today about traditions in vogue in our family. Impossible. Fathers at that time couldn't see their wives or their children in the presence of their own father. Out of modesty. Out of respect. But it came on its own. My father's arms. The only place I felt totally understood. A refuge, yes, of that I am sure. The father. In him, knowledge, love, tenderness, laughter.

Soak in these instants, before, before this terrible thing which I have been skirting since the beginning and that I can't bring myself to say. Not yet.

At home, they also speak French. Often. Her mother whose name is Flower, Zahra, is not quite like her aunts. She wears short, flowery dresses, tight around her very slim waist. She doesn't veil her head and she doesn't have tattoos on her face. All day long, she fills the house with song, with refrains. Lyrics that are still . . . in her head.

"I again see the big sombreros and the mantillas
I hear fandango songs and Seguidilla
*That sing the sede fandango and ség When shines on the plazza . . . the moon . . ."**
Everything is there. The air. The mother's so melodious voice. The sunrays in her eyes and on her face when she looked at the father. Maybe that was happiness. That light. Before.

"But then, can Arabs speak French too?"

To speak a language. To make it your own without losing sight of the fact that it doesn't belong to us. Inextricable suffering. To enter into this certainty. But when? How?

---

* *"Sombreros et mantilles"* ("Sombreros and mantillas") is a 1938 Rina Ketty song that evokes cherished memories. The Italian singer embraced French culture during and slightly before World War II. Her songs nevertheless reflect her Italian roots.

On her grandfather's farm, she goes barefoot to be like her cousins, so numerous that she has a hard time knowing which one is which. But the sole of her foot is fragile, she isn't used to taking her shoes and socks off and the sharp pointy pebbles keep her from running as fast as they do. Is it only because of that that she doesn't share their games? Yet, she doesn't scorn the rag or reed dolls made lovingly by her cousins.

On her grandfather's farm, there are a lot of windowless, dark, barely furnished rooms. Some mattresses and a few woolen rugs woven by her aunts. All of the bedrooms open onto a central courtyard paved with flat stones. The courtyard is huge, filled with bright sunlight, too much sunlight.

But yes, I know, the places are only huge and lit up in children's memories.

In the courtyard, no shady corner, no tree, not even one foot of Virginia creeper, obstinate and spindly, that it is common to find in front of each house in the douars. Dust. Dust. The uneven and dangerous stairs, the crumbling stone walls. No first floor. Roofs . . . but in fact, what did the roofs look like? Pitched? With a terrace? Covered with tiles? Maybe she never looked up, explored what was inaccessible . . . the world stopped at her height. The mere memory of the overheated tiles in the courtyard where no one, not even the children, would run the risk of being during the hottest part of the day. Women's whispers and laughter in the rooms, smells from the kitchen, of roast meat mixed with the smells of manure coming from the cowshed and stables. She is still small enough to sometimes slip into the room reserved for men and share their meal around the low table, sitting between her father and her uncle, despite the prohibition. The women eat in another room, after having served the men.

Where does this very intense impression of freedom come from? Probably from the bare deserted spaces, beyond the wheat fields as far as the eye can see. The echo of children's shouts reverberating far, very far off. Stalk of wheat pulled out, still green, taste of the still young seeds of wheat.

Implacable nudity.

In the shifting light, on the pebbly path, she glimpses her uncle's and her father's silhouettes. First her father. Bare-headed, broad, squat. He wears a suit. Dark pants and jacket, light-colored shirt. His glasses catch flashes of light. A little bit farther back, her uncle. Very wide pants, saroual with multiple folds. Light-colored shirt and white turban. He too. Like her grandfather. All of her uncles, all of the occupants of the farm wear the traditional outfit. But then, how come her father doesn't dress like they do? Why doesn't he live at the farm?

Don't think about that word. Difference. Not yet. Try to keep her balance, her arms outstretched, to go forward slowly.

An inscription, above the big gate, "MIXED BOYS' SCHOOL." They used to say mixed to distinguish these schools from the others, the native schools, reserved for Arabs—she will know that later. That's where she lives. An apartment with a terrace on the second floor. On each side of the vestibule are the bedrooms, the fully equipped all-white kitchen. Their neighbors: other primary school teachers' families. On the same floor. Families with children. After school, she plays in the courtyard with her brothers and Annie, Françoise, Pauline, who are about the same age as she is. She has a big doll, with real hair. A doll given to her in memorable circumstances by a passing inspector, in front of whom she one day recited, without stopping, without making even a single mistake, about ten passages. Forty, her mother says still now, swearing to the gods that she is not exaggerating.

Most often, she is on the terrace. A favorite spot for her exploits and her readings. Precise clear angles. There too, a huge space in her child's eyes, surrounded by walls high enough that she feels protected.

The entire family is settled around the high table. She is sitting between her two brothers, just across from her father, who is watching her. Who is forcing her to eat this red soup with pieces of meat and little bits of vegetables swimming in it. She fills her mouth, spoonful after spoonful. She is afraid of her father's terrible look. Eat! She can't swallow. She has her mouth full. She is choking. In one last effort, she vanquishes her fear, it comes spewing out of her all at once. The consequences? No. Nothing else. She wasn't reprimanded or spanked. She did not hold onto the painful memory of the anger that must have followed. Not even once punished by her father.

The punishments erased? Oh! Here we go, I've got it. The first chink. Maybe the start of an answer to the question. To be punished for a fault that we didn't commit. Or at least for factors beyond our control. These words begin to break through the cocoon carefully woven around memories. Enter into the crux of the memory.

January 1957

At last an anchor. A sure reference point. What could be more solid than a date to support memories? Certified and confirmed by history books. General seven-day strike decreed by the FLN, the National Liberation Front.

The air is glacial. Hand held in her father's, she crosses the village streets. He's the one who has come to pick her up from school for the first time. Usually, at this time, he is still working. He is carrying her little schoolbag where he put back her notebook after noting her class rank. He read it without saying anything. Zero in all subjects. Zero in reading. Zero in dictation. Zero in math. Zero in writing. Rank: 27 out of 27. The teacher gave out the books without saying anything. The other times, she used to announce the ranks, gave pictures to the first three girls, and lectured the ones who didn't get the average. Moment waited for impatiently by the little girl who came running home to announce to her father that she was first. Because she was always first, "the little Muslim girl," as had remarked one of the ticked-off mothers one day as school was letting out.

It's not her fault if this time she is last. She hasn't been to school for the whole week. And it was composition week. The teacher had come in person to their house to warn them. Her father had been inflexible. He didn't teach, didn't send his children to school, obeying the order to the letter. That's all. So he knows well that it's not *her* fault. She is quiet, tries in vain to swallow the bitter lump that comes into her throat. Because she doesn't understand why he decided that she wouldn't go to school. Usually, before the compositions, he's the one who makes her recite the lessons, a formality for her he says often laughing, proud of this child who learns everything very quickly and asks so many questions in order to understand the world.

Let me find the exact nature of my sentiments at that instant. Let me put aside, without concession to the present, the ones that surfaced much later and that are one with everything that has built up within me since, to the point where it is difficult for me to sort them out.

First temptation, to tell about her grief. Tears. To even add to them. The fear of punishment, too. That seems so obvious! But no. Nothing about all that.

There is also this word that imposes itself with such strength that it makes me throw out all the others: humiliation. First humiliation. So strong, so unacceptable that it determined all the rest. My life. But this word is too difficult to be thought of by a child. Too heavy. The first experience of injustice seems more adequate to me. First step on a long and painful learning experience.

". . . because we're Arabs."

In the middle of the empty lot across from the school, her father stops. They are almost at their house. He takes his daughter in his arms. Hugs her very tightly. She has her face right up against his, arms around his neck. He talks. She listens. Avidly. She grasps the words, captures them, forever. For later on. As if she knows that that instant would not be followed by any more like it.

*To retrieve my father's words now. I immediately perceive
their softness, the desire to convince me by looking for the right
words. His words . . . anchored in me. Forever.*

War. Enemies. French. Arabs. Liberation. She has to know.
Under the same sun, men make war on each other. He and
those he is close to are fighting so as to no longer be humiliated. To have the right to be free on a land which belongs to
them. Let's go! This man so strong, so fair, feared by all of his
students, respected by his colleagues, a humiliated man? Too
difficult to accept. She lets herself soak in all these words said
softly, gravely, without hatred exactly. She listens to him until the end, without asking questions that are running through
her mind.

She opens her eyes wide, looks for war around her, in these
so peaceful places. Here, these men who walk with a slow step,
these children running down the street playing on a skate-
board, these women who were chatting a little while ago near
the school, and all the others in the village, all the ones she saw
every day, all of them are at war? No, she sees nothing. But she
believes him, and knows that in this instant, her life just turned
upside down, even if in the following days, she reveals nothing
about it.

She ends up asking a question, just one, "can I keep playing
with Annie, Françoise, and Pauline?"

She keeps playing with them. But from now on, she looks
at it differently. She knows that she is not quite like them. She
wants to understand, grasp the differences, the difference.
She observes and listens to everything that is being said with a
new acuity.

On her grandfather's farm, men come sometimes at night
and shut themselves up with her father and uncles in the big
center room, for hours. They make a lot of noise with their
clunky shoes, and she hears them talking. She has trouble sleeping now. The women call them *brothers* among themselves,
lowering their voices. In the morning, when the children wake
up, the *brothers* have gone.

I never saw them. Only the noise of voices resounds in my memory, heavy dragging feet, and the creaking of doors closed behind them.

February 7, 1957

That night, war erupted in her house while everyone slept. It appeared as men in uniform and with weapons. French soldiers accompanied by a man with his head covered by a black balaclava, a man whom her father addressed in Arabic and whose name he repeated several times with astonishment. They entered their house in the middle of the night. Two of them shut themselves in the living room with her father. She heard what they were saying. Network, cell, *fellaga*. They were speaking loudly. So loudly that her little brother, a baby, woke up and started to cry. Her mother, in tears, came and went in the bedroom, cradling him so that he stopped shouting. Petrified, hugging each other fearfully, the children were watching.

There were five of them. They wrecked everything. They were certainly looking for something. They threw her father's notebooks on the ground, his books, and even her books. They opened the armoires, emptied the closets, ripped open the mattresses, the bags of white flour, semolina, and lentils, they went through everything but they didn't find anything.

Then they left, taking her father. Her mother was crying so much that, so as not to start crying herself, the little girl started to put away and pick up the papers. Then they all took refuge in the big unmade bed.

Of the two following days, I have no memory.

Then, shattering the wait, in the torpor of the afternoon, there was her mother's cry. There were her howls. Her curses. And, very quickly, the departure for another village. Another house.

Still other words: torture, execution, death. And still later on, martyr. But above all, absence.

They go farther off on the path. My father, my uncles executed on the same day are no longer anything more than indistinct silhouettes in my shaky memory.

Later, years later, she will go pray on the grave. A mass grave, a simple tumulus with no flower or tombstone. Bare. Implacable bareness.

THE LITTLE GIRL FROM THE SLUM WITHOUT A NAME

She could have been named Ariane. Why Ariane? Because of her name, and also because of labyrinths. Of the sort that we have to go through since childhood, for a long time, until we find the light.

She could have been born in a real house, with white walls, with big windows always open on a garden overflowing with roses and lilacs, beds covered with flowered linen and everywhere the smell of chocolate cake. To have flowy hair, strewn with these white flowers more transparent than immortals, firefly eyes to light up the too dark days and vine-like fingers to wrap around the ones she would have loved. She could have grasped little golden and dancing flames in her mother's gaze each time her eyes met hers. To have a father taller than trees there, even more solid, with thousands of roots to sink into the earth and never get taken out again.

She could have been born ten years earlier or a hundred twenty years later and continue to live for a long time, a very long time after her death, never to disappear, like the stars that keep on shining even though they are dead; since stars die too. Only their light hangs on infinitely, up there, all the way up there, so as not to turn the sky into another desert.

Later on, she would have learned how to walk, first tottering, and then step by step, often falling to be lifted up again, coddled, consoled. Lift her arms to be picked up, and point her finger at each thing before naming it. And then to stammer, first to try it out, and then to be heard, to be listened to, to be understood. To learn everything that adults want you to learn to become a real little girl with long hair brushed each morning by light, soft hands, Queen Anne's lace collars smelling clean and red shoes, with real whims sometimes satisfied, with real griefs always appeased and wondering looks bigger than the sky, bigger than the sea, ceaselessly renewed.

Then she will have discovered, alone maybe, slowly maybe, but surely, oh yes, surely, some of the elements that compose our life: water, the confident light of days, the words written in books and music.

So, she would have grown up. Maybe not too quickly to conserve as long as possible the power we have, as a child, over all our loved ones. But she would have grown up with her eyes wide open so as not to let the least crumb of happiness escape.

But, how do we grow up when we are born in a shack of sheet metal and wood, set on a wasteland in the middle of the projects with no name?

As for her, her name is Rania.

She was born on a day of whipping winds, and no one on that day heard her mother's moans. No one heard her first cry. But maybe she didn't cry out.

She doesn't know her father. He went away on a boat to look for oblivion in another country, for such a long time that she too has forgotten his face, his voice, his name.

The sea is not far. And the gulls often come to sit on the landfill on the edge of the projects with no name. She never saw it, but she hears its waves in her head, each time that she closes her eyes to sleep. Sometimes, on stormy days, the surf is so loud that it almost manages to cover the rain drumming on the zinc roof and in the tubs set in front of the door. All these water noises in syncopated rhythm, it's her music, a music which beats for her for a long time at the heart of the night.

All that she wants is to be able to go away one day in her turn.

She looks around her, ceaselessly; she looks at women, men, other children. She listens to them too, but she can't manage to understand what they are saying, what they are playing at, what they are dreaming of; by the way, she doesn't even know if they are dreaming. And their words aren't like the ones she invents for herself all alone. So she decided to be quiet.

No one knows why, as she grows, her eyes take on the color of seaweed, becoming more and more transparent. But no one in the projects ever saw seaweed. The stones all around only have the color of stone, of rust.

Nor does she know why she often dreams of labyrinths. Of huge, dark, damp halls, tirelessly tread over in useless comings and goings. Every night, she runs, banks, gets lost in inextricable mazes, because no one stretched a thread out for her to help her come out into the light.

Every morning, when she wakes, the light is there, it comes through the gaps of the badly nailed boards and scratches on the sheet metal roofs. She doesn't even need to open her eyes to know that the sun is there, that it sets the air on fire that she breathes in the windowless room. She has to get up very quickly to go look for water. With her, her mother doesn't even have to shout to be obeyed.

Rania always takes the same plastic jerry cans: the blue one and the green one. She sometimes has to go several kilometers and has to knock at several doors before finding a place to fill them up. The security guard at the factory and oil refinery, next door, sometimes has enough of all the turbulent children from the slum without a name who come, one after the other, to ask for water, and who squabble each day in front of the gate. Sometimes he doesn't answer their calls. She knows that she must at all costs bring back water to the house, if not they won't have any to make something to eat and to do their laundry. So, day after day, she goes a little farther, farther and farther. Her arms hurt a little when she comes back, but she doesn't complain. To whom would she go to complain? And then there is the lapping of the water that keeps pace with her all the way down the path. That's enough for her. It's a little bit like the first notes of her nightly music.

Rania goes to school sometimes, on the other side of the
walls of the projects. To do as the others do. She has neither
notebook nor a schoolbag. But she sneaks in the middle of
the children and she comes in without making herself noticed.
There are so many children in the classrooms, so much noise
and turbulence that they don't even notice that she is there.
Sitting in the back of the classroom, she listens and watches;
the pronounced words reach her, she picks up a few for later,
you never know, but once they have cleared a path to her consciousness, to the meaning, they stay stuck in her throat and
refuse to come out. The other children repeat, write, recite
and catcall at the same time. In all this tumult, they don't
look at her, they don't call on her. Because they think she
is imprisoned in her silence, that she is surrounded by glass
walls. It's as if she didn't exist. From time to time, she takes
a book, flips through it, looks at the pictures for a long time.
There are little girls in Queen Anne's lace–collared dresses and
houses with big open windows and roofs with red tile. Fathers,
there permanently, who, standing on the doorstep, place their
hand on their child's head. The words in the books are black
and silent, they slither like snakes and don't resound in her
head, even when she traces the outlines with her fingers or with
a stick on the ground, sometimes, when she is alone under the
tree behind the shack.

She could have kept on living for a long time behind those
glass walls, in the slum without a name, with eyes becoming
ever more transparent and, louder and louder, the water's music in her head. But maybe it is in the effort of tracing characters
in the dust that she found the path of dreams. Or the effort of
watching the stars that have long since disappeared. No one in
the projects knows why, one morning, she was no longer there.
No one ever looked for her either.

She has now gone to the other side of her dream. There,
thousands of little girls with flowy hair mixed in with white
flowers more transparent than immortals and with creeper

fingers hold each other's hands and sing. In the middle of the circle, a tree unfolds its branches very high in the sky. In each girl's firefly eyes shine stars captured on the day's threshold, just before the call to prayer.

No one else but them hears their song. It is only a slight breath of air, a respiration that moves forward with the morning, with the light, crosses the walls separating beings, spreads out over the still-sleeping city and slips into the heart of each house. A slight breath, a caress, scarcely quiver which suddenly lends iridescence to dreams. All of the dreams that give men the elusive taste of happiness.

AFTERWORD

Alison Rice

Backgrounds and Beginnings

Maïssa Bey is the pseudonym that Samia Benameur adopted in order to protect her identity when her first novel, *Au commencement était la mer,* went to press in 1996 in the midst of a civil war in the author's Algerian homeland. An erudite woman who had been content theretofore to focus on her roles as a high school French teacher and a married mother of four, she suddenly felt compelled to put pen to paper for publication when one of her fellow teachers was murdered. This colleague was unfortunately far from the only innocent individual to lose his life in this period that came to be known in French as *la décennie noire,* a dark decade marked by countless assassinations, including those of intellectuals and professionals, women and men, who were struck down because they dared to express their thoughts. This violent civil war broke out almost exactly thirty years after the close of the Algerian War for Independence that brought an end to French colonial domination in this land. Maïssa Bey was only six years old when her father lost his life in the first conflict, and she has forever been affected by this tragedy.

In her very first publication, the aforementioned 1996 novel, Maïssa Bey broached such contentious topics as abortion and stoning in an exposition of the constraints placed on women in Algeria, especially in the context of the civil war, when groups of Islamic fundamentalists were unbending in their will to wrest control of the country from the military-based secular government. After publishing a collection of short stories in 1998, *Nouvelles d'Algérie,* that continued to tell the tales of her female compatriots, the writer came out with an award-winning second novel, *Cette fille-là,* in 2001 that grappled with the many ways religion and society work together in Algeria to stifle women and to ostracize in special ways those who show any sign of divergence from the norm.

It was in 2002, the year the civil war came to an end in Algeria, that the gripping narrative *Entendez-vous dans les montagnes* . . . (*Do You Hear in the Mountains* . . .) was first published at the esteemed French publishing house Éditions de l'Aube, where Maïssa Bey had already become an established author. Two years later, the short-story collection *Sous le jasmin la nuit* (*Under the Jasmine at Night*) was made available to a growing readership by the same prestigious publisher. These two publications represent a crucial turning point in the author's career, as the conclusion of the second violent war she had experienced firsthand in her homeland allowed her to embark upon textual explorations of her father's fate during the first conflict. Working under the label of fiction enabled the writer to delve unselfconsciously into her past and to indulge her imagination in order to relate difficult events and resuscitate dormant memories.

In the years since the appearance in print of *Do You Hear in the Mountains* . . . and *Under the Jasmine at Night,* Maïssa Bey has continued to publish in the prolific vein that marked these early efforts as a writer, and her notoriety has grown exponentially. Now the author of a variety of novels, critical essays, collections of short stories, and works for the theater, she has arguably become the most sought-after woman writer of Algeria. Her work is frequently the subject of doctoral theses around the world, and she is regularly invited to give lectures and participate in interviews in diverse settings. Her 2005 novel *Surtout ne te retourne pas* was translated into English as *Above All, Don't Look Back* and published by the University of Virginia Press in 2009, making her writing accessible to an even wider readership. This is quite a feat for a woman whose literary career began in a country that offered few, if any, publishing opportunities.

When Maïssa Bey completed her first novel in the mid-1990s, she had to seek a publisher in France because there were no publishing houses in Algeria to which she could submit her manuscript. The situation has changed since then, however, and although the author has remained faithful to Éditions de l'Aube, which has published so many of her works, she has also committed these same books to Éditions Barzakh, a publishing house that was created in Algeria in 2000 as the violence of the civil war was waning. Éditions Barzakh features other highly successful French-language authors from Algeria who are writing today, such as Kaouther Adimi and Kamel Daoud, and their work is thereby known and appreciated in their home country as well as in France. Interestingly enough, Maïssa Bey also participated in founding a publishing house in the southern French city of Montpellier alongside three other women with ties to Algeria in the very same year, 2000. This publishing house, Chèvre-feuille étoilée, has focused since its inception on providing a forum for women's expression, and it has sought to distribute works written by women not only in France but also, especially, in Algeria, as well as elsewhere.

The development of this publishing house is only one example of a number of proactive measures that Maïssa Bey has taken in her quest to make a difference in ways that extend beyond her own well-crafted text. In 2001, she cofounded Paroles et écriture, an organization in Algeria that encourages women to come together and express themselves through embracing both conversation and written composition in their gatherings. The innovative work and testimonies that have emerged thanks to these meetings have been published in a journal, *Étoiles d'encre,* that is available to readers on both sides of the Mediterranean. A complementary initiative entailed the establishment of a library that is also a cultural center, a sorely needed place of exchange and enlightenment that has enhanced the lives of many individuals since its 2005 opening in the town of Sidi-Bel-Abbès, where Maïssa Bey has lived since she was a teenager. These initiatives go hand in hand with the writer's vision for her own work as capable of bringing about change in Algerian society. Literature, in her view, should not be located in an ivory tower but instead should be accessible to all, both in its creation and in its consumption.

In her spoken comments as well as her written reflections,

Maïssa Bey often emphasizes her passion for reading. She regularly cites well-known authors from her homeland ranging from Albert Camus to Mohammed Dib among the many influences on her work, but another name inevitably comes up as well, that of her literary forebear Assia Djebar, whose books Bey devoured when she was in her early teens. In 2005, this brilliant predecessor became the first woman from the African continent to be elected to the Académie Française, the illustrious institution made up of writers and intellectuals who convene in the heart of the French capital. Always quick to pay homage to this groundbreaking Algerian woman writer who provided her with such inspiration from early on, Bey is clearly indebted to the advances Djebar made, especially when it came to exposing the experiences of women in literary form. But she has also been able to bring unique perspectives to her written work, adopting angles of approach that reveal the fact that her itinerary—unlike that of Djebar and a number of other well-known francophone women writers from her country—has not included extended stays in or definitive moves to other locations but has instead been characterized by a steady presence in the place of her birth, even during the dangerous decade when she first began to publish her work.

Her ongoing residence in Algeria gives an ever-evident urgency to Bey's writing, and while nostalgia and melancholy make an appearance in her work, they inevitably intermingle with the immediacy of the imminent, revealing movements that mark the present in her land. The author is deeply aware of the current challenges that characterize her country, and she is well positioned to take on problematic issues from the perspective of the citizen who is struggling in her daily life, along with others. What emerges with particular strength in the two works juxtaposed in the preceding pages is the ways in which the past and present are inseparable. The war raging in Algeria during the 1990s is inextricably tied to the war the Algerians were waging against the French between 1954 and 1962 in an effort to gain freedom from long-standing colonial rule. That bloody conflict, which resulted in the independence of the Algerian people after more than 130 years of French domination, is brought to bear on the more recent conflict in undeniable ways in both of the texts in this volume.

Born in 1950, Maïssa Bey was just a small child when the first war broke out, and she endured her father's death at the hands of the French for his membership in the anticolonial guerrilla movement, the National Liberation Front, known by the acronym FLN, early on in the struggle. This traumatic loss when she was so young engraved many of the war's details in her mind and made it an important part of her oeuvre. What is remarkable is that, even though her life and work have been profoundly influenced by the shock of such unforgettable formative experiences, her texts have nonetheless represented neither a wallowing in grief nor a desire to communicate a grievance. Instead, her writings have embodied a special form of forgiveness that at once attempts to truly see others, whatever their background, and to appropriately articulate a variety of personal histories, all while according special attention to the oft-overlooked details of the lives of women.

Interestingly enough, her early exposure to immense violence and heartbreaking sorrow undoubtedly reinforced Bey's natural inclination for literary composition. Even if she didn't become a published writer until she was in her forties, she was arguably predisposed to a career in literature, for her father's initiation into the world of letters and her ensuing passion for reading meant that long before she became a writer, she was drawn to the contemplation of words.

The Gift of the Gaze:
Do You Hear in the Mountains . . .

Maïssa Bey's striking *Do You Hear in the Mountains . . .* isn't easy to categorize according to genre. Upon first glance, it is tempting to jump to the conclusion that this is an autobiographical text, especially since documents from the life of the writer's father frame the narrative, setting the tone for a factual reading. The photograph featured within the work, situated right after the title page, contains a caption stating that this is "the only picture of Maïssa's father" and indicating that the image dates back to the "summer of 1955" as further evidence of its authenticity. The presence of the father in this image, and the clear connection to the author that is established through the use of her first name, set the tone for an approach to the text that seeks continuity between lived experience and the story related therein. But the train ride toward Marseilles that a middle-aged Algerian woman embarks upon in the company of an older Frenchman and a young Frenchwoman is entirely imagined. The freedom afforded through fiction enables the author to create a scenario that brings together three characters from different generations and diverging experiences in order to tackle head-on the horrific circumstances of her father's execution and contemplate the complexities of the conflict that was the Algerian War.

The first dedication of this text is to her father, the one "who will never be able to read these lines" because he is deceased, not because he is illiterate, as is the case for the parents of some postcolonial francophone writers. The portrait the author paints of her father in this work is that of a highly educated individual, a product of the French educational system whose command of the colonizer's language is perfect, even down to his accent. As Bey has often attested, it was thanks to her father that she began to read and write as a young girl, that she acquired these skills that she has always associated with his influence on her life. A brief three words follow the initial dedication to the father, in which the author mentions her sons, thereby establishing from the outset the possibility of lineage and implicitly pointing toward hope. Perhaps the sons can read this poignant text, feel pride in their grandfather's courage, and take his story to heart, accepting it as an important part of their familial inheritance. The second epigraph points toward another type of inheritance, as it consists of an evocative quotation from a poem composed by one of the greatest French writers of all time, Victor Hugo: These verses highlight questions of race and colonial conquest and indicate that such issues have long been a part of the French literary tradition. The "passive obedience" to which the poem's title makes reference carries particular import for more recent contemplations of responsibility in the aftermath of war in different contexts, for the ruminations regarding "orders" and "obedience" that are at the forefront of the principal protagonist's mind in the text are also central to the novel that this character is reading.

A brief passage from this other book figures in Bey's narrative very early on, as the protagonist who is reading is aware that her impressions in the present situation are impacted by the words she sees on the page before her. When the narrative voice calls attention to the act of reading in the opening paragraphs of the text in this manner, it inspires those who hold Bey's book in their hands to think about the ways in which their own reading experience is at once influenced by their surroundings and exerts an influence on their perception of those surroundings.

It is not an accident that the italicized phrases selected from this other text to appear within quotation marks in *Do You Hear in the Mountains* ... begin with the words "I was observing him." The first-person narrative voice from this intertextual reference is closely examining someone else, scrutinizing an individual with gray hair. In a similar manner, the woman in Bey's text is staring at the man with whom she will share the close quarters of the train compartment in the hours ahead. If hair color in this instance gives a clue as to age, then it may also provide some insight into this person's possible past. The man across from her may have been old enough to have participated in heinous acts in her country forty years earlier, and a similar connection to possible wrongdoing in war makes age a theme of significance in the book the woman is holding. It isn't until later that the identity of this aptly titled novel, *The Reader,* is revealed when the male protagonist picks it up and hands it back to its owner after it has fallen to the floor. Although the contents of this novel are not addressed in Bey's narrative, the 1995 best-selling book by the German law professor Bernhard Schlink has known such resounding international success that many readers will immediately recognize it as a work that probes how later generations should appropriately come to terms with the wrongs their countrymen committed in conflicts that preceded them. Those who are familiar with

The Reader's delicate treatment of such difficult questions as accountability and justice following the atrocities of the Holocaust know that its mere mention sets the stage for the establishment of powerful parallels for those who survived or were born in the wake of the Algerian War.

While this reference to *The Reader* is made explicit in this work, another important publication with strong resonance for Bey's narrative remains implicit throughout, and that is Jean-Paul Sartre's celebrated play *Huis clos*. The original title of this well-known theatrical work is a French legal term that refers to a private discussion behind closed doors. While the English translation of the title, *No Exit,* loses some of the implications of the French expression, it nonetheless communicates the sense of being shut up in a confined space without hope for escape. Sartre's play portrays three main characters—a man, a woman, and a younger woman—who are stuck in a situation that forces them to confront each other, and their respective pasts, and to come to the realization that relationships with others can constitute a form of torture, a version of hell, especially when there is no way to elude the others' persistent stare, their ever-present penetrating gaze. It is no accident that Sartre composed this play in 1943 and 1944, the final two years of the Second World War, and that he was grappling with questions such as individual and collective identity, responsibility, and freedom in this context.

Sartre's plays are sometimes associated with "the theater of the absurd," a category of works by such playwrights as Samuel Beckett and Eugène Ionesco that tended to do away with various theatrical conventions such as the classical unities of action, place, and time. Although Maïssa Bey's work initially appears to adhere to these Aristotelian rules for drama given that the action is focused on the train compartment and doesn't exceed twenty-four hours, geographical constraints are not strictly respected as the train in which the three central characters are traveling through the French countryside covers a considerable distance. Bey's text bears an additional likeness to theatrical works of the absurd in its conscious use of ellipses, for such punctuation highlights the ways in which language is unable to fully represent the complexities of human experience. Also, the third-person narrative voice addresses the contrived nature of the meeting of these three individuals in a cleverly conceived metatextual passage, emphasizing the "situation's absurdity" and exclaiming that "someone could even write a play about it," hinting at the similarities between this work and the theater of this tradition.

This unlikely coming together of three people who represent diverse relationships to the Algerian War could have led to entirely different results. There is little that predisposes them to opening themselves up to a real conversation in 1996 about the combat that had occurred across the Mediterranean Sea forty years earlier, especially since they are from such different backgrounds: the former French soldier, the daughter of an Algerian martyr, and the granddaughter of a *pied-noir,* a Frenchman who was born and raised in Algeria. These travelers easily could have opted to keep silent, as so many have in the wake of this conflict. In fact, the two older individuals agree that this is a possibility, a "right" as he claims, or as she articulates it, perhaps the "only recourse" or "the only remedy" that serves to "protect" those who were deeply affected by the war. At the time of this conversation, the French nation has certainly erred on the side of silence, refusing to name the war until 1999 and eliding its occurrence in many textbooks; in Algeria, no alternative is available to the official version of events dictated by the war's heroes, as the woman explains in the narrative. A real verbal exchange was especially improbable in France, a country in which people do not acknowledge each other, as the woman laments when neither of her fellow travelers bothers to greet her: "Rare are those who trouble themselves to look at and greet strangers." The foreigner finds this tendency to ignore others particularly peculiar and struggles to adjust to "not existing in others' eyes." But within the confines of the train compartment, a catalyst leads to conversation when another figure penetrates this private space for a brief moment to relate what she believes she has witnessed.

The sudden intrusion of a woman from the first-class section of the train into their seating area serves to free these individuals from an elaborate game in which they seem only to look at others when their eyes are closed or to steal a glance when they are safely insulated through reflections off the window. This fourth passenger, who claims that thugs have attempted to steal suitcases, provides an indication of the attackers' ethnicity based on their appearance: "Arabs, I'm sure! I saw them!" She repeats her pronouncement on their guilt before leaving the compartment as precipitously as she had entered it, in a fit of concern about her belongings. This rush to judgment is especially disturbing because of the accuser's focus on racial designations and what she considers to be predictable profiles. This egregious embrace of negative stereotypes prompts the older man, who has thus far avoided meeting her eyes, to finally look right at the woman seated across from him, and this connection marks a turning point in their interaction. Conversation follows.

While the language doesn't flow in long, elegant sentences that make up well-developed paragraphs, the dialogue that transpires allows for a great deal of meaning to be made among the three participants. What begins as polite recognition of the others in their midst turns into a discussion they must not abandon before they have taken it to its conclusion. It is interesting that this text has been adapted as a play because it is at once intensely concentrated on inner thoughts, on recollections and impressions, and innately theatrical, easily imaginable as a staged set of exchanges between three people heading nonchalantly toward the sea who are suddenly confronted with a painful past. In many senses, the discussion that takes place during the trip is between the older man and the middle-aged woman as they bring up specific places and dates that they have in common. We have little insight into the younger woman's personal reactions, whereas the third-person narrator gives access to the thoughts and memories of the woman and regularly, in italicized text, plunges into the mind of the man. But the teenager who knows little about the Algerian War plays a crucial role in this conversation because she gives balance and presents an external perspective, serving as a pretext for explanations that

would seem unnecessary to the narrative if she weren't a part
of it.

What the Algerian woman strives to find in her older interloc-
utor is something she has sought since her father was murdered
during her childhood: A face-to-face encounter with his assas-
sin. This is what this scenario enacts, a seemingly impossible
exchange that ignores legal and social barriers and brings together *individuals* who were affected by a situation over which
they had little control. The French veteran calmly allows early
in the conversation that there were those who "gave orders"
and those who "executed" them out of "duty" or "obligatory
obedience." It is later that he becomes more emotional, and
he is forced to exclaim as tensions mount that even if he was
among those who were only following orders, he was not unaf-
fected by his actions: "No one got out of this war unscathed!
No one! You hear!" Bey beautifully communicates the truth
that, even if he is the embodiment of her father's torturer, this
character is not the enemy in this text but is instead a relatively
well-rounded protagonist who demonstrates thoughtfulness
and empathy, and through whom the woman gains access to
her father in important ways. His memory of her close relative as "tranquil and debonair," qualities that are "Astonishing
for an Arab!," flies in the face of the stereotypes that still
abound and serves as a strong response to the assertions of
the woman from the first-class car. His reminiscences serve to
individuate her father in the face of generalizations like those
that provided the French with the ammunition they needed to
carry out menacing measures during the Algerian War, clichés
encapsulated in such phrases as "all terrorists are fearsome."
Rather than allowing others to succumb to these assumptions,
the woman at the heart of this text seems to be asking for
a gesture of recognition, a movement of appreciation that, in a
flashback, her father's torturer cannot help but carry out when
the man before him "finally raises his head and looks at Jean,
right in the eyes."

The author of this text has striven to restore dignity and
humanity to her father, who was stripped of these qualities in

the eyes of the French on the occasion of his cowardly killing. She has done so in part by attributing to him a noble set of final acts that are in line with his official designation as a martyr, as a man who sacrificed all for the greater good of his country's liberation. He withstood torture, refusing to provide the names of others who were complicit with his efforts as a member of the National Liberation Front. In this instance, her father embraced a silence with an entirely different meaning from the one that has characterized the attitudes in both France and Algeria in the aftermath of war; he stood firm in his courageous decision *not* to talk, *not* to fill in the blanks, *not* to denounce others, even at the cost of his life. The imagined details of his final actions in this text allow Bey to provide her father with a dignified end that is complemented at the conclusion of the work by a collection of four documents that produce proof of his life, attesting to his official birthdate and his French nationality; his moral standing and conduct; his level of education and appointment as a teacher. Like the photograph of the man with his daughters at its opening, the text closes with a personal touch: A postcard containing the careful, attentive writing of the dutiful family man. The father, whose name does not appear at any point in the narrative, is repeatedly named in these paratextual apparatuses and is provided with a certain legitimacy through the presence of these documents that authenticate his achievements and corroborate his character. It is noteworthy that the Algerian woman is not given a name in the text either, whereas the older man and the young woman both bear typically French first names, Jean and Marie respectively. Rather than stripping her of her identity, this anonymity bestows upon this character a flexibility that enables her to slip between various designators, those of author and narrator and protagonist, allowing for a variety of viewpoints that come through in a text that isn't stable and sedentary but always moving in its ongoing exploration of a plethora of perspectives. This doesn't lead to closure, for the loose ends of this story will never be neatly tied up, but it does contribute to "something" becoming "unknotted" in this unnamed Algerian woman, creating a dénouement in a text that exemplifies not a judgment or a reckoning but, instead, an act of profound forgiveness.

In an ultimate gesture of generosity toward the other opposite her, toward the man whom she has accorded such careful attention over the preceding hours, the woman permits him to have the last word. His final, faltering assertions affirm what she has suspected all along, that he was in the presence of her father just before he died. He admits this, confessing his role through a revelation with deep significance for the woman in her very being: She resembles her father, both in her look and, more pertinently, in her way of looking. She has always longed to look like him in these two senses of the expression, in her appearance as well as her manner, and the man has perceived this desire and fulfilled it in a punch line that couldn't have been spoken if she hadn't first opened up to him in an unprecedented present. The woman had endeavored ever since she was a little girl "to put a face on the men who had tortured and finished off her father," but she had only managed to picture them as faceless "monsters" with no human traits whatsoever. Now, however, as the train arrives at its destination, she has realized that "executioners have a man's face," "hands," and "at times even a man's reactions and nothing allows them to be distinguished from others." Rather than serving as a reassuring awareness, this is a terrifying lesson that is integral to the book that she didn't have time to finish on this trip. Despite her fear, she takes the time to absorb the man she has for so long tried to envisage: "Face to face, the man and the woman do not move." She doesn't hope for any major transformation, on either a personal or a public level, at a time when war is once again leading to widespread murder in her homeland and she has ironically come as a refugee to claim protection in the land of her former enemy, but she doesn't shy away from this confrontation: "She looks at him, she observes him, she analyzes him, attentively, minutely, as if she wanted to fix each feature of his face in her memory." By fully examining his features, by truly taking in his look, she has granted him a form of absolution that is communicated through the gift of the gaze.

Ways with Words: *Under the Jasmine at Night*

In her 2004 collection of short stories, the writer continues her quest to render in written form the experiences of women from her homeland. Her hope to create narratives that enable a variety of voices to be heard necessarily comes up against the inadequacy of the words these women have at their disposal. In the first short story, "Under the Jasmine at Night," Maya eschews the adjective "unhappy" as she seeks to describe the sentiment that characterizes her daily life, actively wondering "how to put into words" why she feels the way she does, "so dry, arid, impenetrable, unfeeling." No one thing is clearly at fault for her "malaise," though the "masks that she never removes" and the expectations for "submissiveness" among women in her society appear to play a large role in her dissatisfaction. In the end, it is not a set of coherent, well-formulated sentences that emerge from this woman but instead a "slow howl that comes out of her," almost against her own will, but that "shatters" the "silences" that surround her, the silences that paradoxically seek to silence her. This sustained lament from a female protagonist who is so profoundly preoccupied that she hardly realizes that she is making noise is reminiscent of the cry that Assia Djebar describes in her 1984 novel *L'Amour, la fantasia* as escaping from the mouth of an Algerian-born woman without her conscious awareness as she walks through the streets of Paris at night.

In a similar incident found in the third short story, "In Good Faith upon My Honor," the woman's voice falters when she wishes to tell her husband to leave, "and a bizarre sound" slips out, "something like a gurgle or a moan," a surprising noise for the man who expected a cry or a scream. But this indescribable sound communicates a deeply felt shock at the news he has just unveiled, and it hints at an intense form of mourning. The female protagonist has learned that her significant other is taking on a second wife, and in this moment of revelation, it is the final brief word in a string of syllables that slams into her, hitting her like a slap, and making her greatest fear hit home, since "his words" "gave an unbearable reality" to the pronouncement that she would have to adjust to another woman in the household. She lights upon the right word to describe her temporary paralysis, as she perceives that she is "petrified" and takes some joy in the aptness of the term. She realizes that she is a "statue," unable to move because of the inflexibility of her society's expectations. She is always compelled to fulfill "responsibilities," while he is continually exempt from culpability: "The only guilty parties are women who refuse to submit to the laws." What shakes her from a moment of "revolt" in which she "seizes a knife" and appears to be on the verge of committing an act of irrevocable violence is another screech. This time it is not she who cries out but an infant, her own child, and this offspring she had desired for so long brings her back to her sense of purpose. She is reminded of her own mother, of all the others who came before her and who suffered similar fates, and she shifts her focus to the baby she scoops up in her arms, once again resigned to the roles assigned to her for this little girl's sake. The mother in this story has no choice but to "utter the words" that are not hers but that have been dictated to her, prescripted through her "duty as a Muslim woman" in a country where 99 percent of the population is of this religious faith. Women in Algeria have long been considered to be minors, a status that was made official when the Family Code became law in 1984, and they have very little opportunity to stand up to tradition and propose other ways of living in this environment.

When the woman in the third short story employs such words as "submissive" to explain the attitude expected of her, she seems to be anticipating the comments of Leïla, a prospective stage actor who delivers a monologue in an audition in the fourth short story, "Improvisations." This Algerian-born woman who is trying out for a part in France makes comments about her appearance and competency in French in self-reflective statements that are reminiscent of some of the thoughts attributed to the Algerian woman in *Do You Hear in the Mountains . . .* as she ponders her place in the country of the former colonizer and wonders how evident it is that she hails from elsewhere. Leïla asks aloud why the advertisement for this role indicated that they were "seeking a fragile woman," and she specifically questions what "fragile" means, pointing out how such ideas of daintiness, docility, and weakness lead women to continually assume roles that are not at all natural but that cater to men who need to feel that they can protect those who are less strong than they are. Leïla brings up words that she labels "interesting" because their supposed meanings are so often taken for granted and yet they are seldom as simple as they seem, such as "choice" and "happy," terms that she reveals are "changeable" and carry definitions that are "circumstantial." The final expression that she seeks to highlight during this impromptu speech is a word that she explains is untranslatable, referring in her mother tongue to "those who no longer have souls, no more roots, no more memory," to those who have done everything they can to assimilate into another culture, to perform perfectly in an adopted tongue, even though they have run the "risk of losing themselves" in the effort. The irony is that even though she has retained the concept, she has forgotten this very word and therefore is the living embodiment of the person who has sacrificed all to become someone else, an integrated immigrant who has left behind everything from her former life.

In an interview, Bey asserts that the effect that the concomitant activities of reading and writing had during her childhood and adolescence was indispensable, for they allowed her not only to survive but to thrive. As she puts it, "words taught [her] to decipher the world," since "naming" things provided them with a sense of "reality." With time, she learned to "transform appearances" and make up for what she perceived to be missing in "reality" through "fragments of fiction." This capacity that writing has to transform the world and transport the reader comes through in the fifth short story, "If, on a Summer's Night . . . ," especially in the poetic proclivities of one of the seven sisters who go up to the rooftop on a sleepless night: "she has the strange and fascinating compulsion to let herself be too easily carried away by the magic of words, to let them flow out of her without ever looking to hold them back, believing thus to act on the ugliness of the world." Another sister is enlivened by the power of words: "Do you know that when I read, when I write, when I let the words come to me, all that surrounds me disappears?" This disabled young woman is no longer dejected about her deformity, since she "can thus imagine taking possession of the world and molding it in her way," as the consequences of her love for words are depicted in this text whose title takes liberties with a complex, self-reflexive 1979 novel by the Italian author Italo Calvino.

In the heartrending portrayal of "The Little Girl from the Slum without a Name" in the final short story of this collection, the child "born in a shack of sheet metal and wood, set on a wasteland in the middle of the projects" cannot find similar solace, for the simple reason that she is illiterate. Even in the aural arena, she can't understand others when she ventures beyond the borders of her hovel for "their words aren't like the ones she invents for herself." So when she encounters printed letters in books, in the school where she has had to sneak in, these words "are black and silent, they slither like snakes and don't resound in her head," and she remains at a loss, forever removed from the meanings that the other children are making in this educational space. For this little girl, words have fallen short, she has failed to connect to them and through them, and in the end she has recourse to song, to sounds far from words but that have led to a beauty beyond, to dreams that provide a hint of happiness, if only for a brief moment.

The passage from life to death is addressed in the second short story, "On This Last Morning," and the irony of this momentous event is that it is "as if she had been dead for a long time" due to the absence of passion in her life. The son, who examines his mother's facial features for the very first time on the day of her passing, wonders if she had ever known the meaning of the word "peace." She may not have, but it is clear in a delightful depiction of her multiple pregnancies that this woman knew "glory" through the experience of giving birth, at least the seven times that led to male progeny.

The specificity of raising female children in Algerian society is conveyed with conviction in the eighth short story, titled "Nowhybecause." For the family portrayed in these pages, words do not necessarily align in a satisfactory manner but instead often hang there inconclusively, as the opening dialogues demonstrate: "Because. Period. Silence." Words turn out in such instances to be concrete obstacles to communication, going against their very definitions to serve in this fashion: "Because: subordinating conjunction. Followed, under normal circumstances, by a phrase that books and teachers call: causal subordinate clause. With a verb in the indicative." This may be the official way that grammar works, but in the microcosm of this household, language functions entirely differently: "in our family, the causes are so indisputable that the clauses are deleted, straightaway. We only function through ellipses." The ellipses that abound in *Do You Hear in the Mountains . . .* are therefore present as a rule in these familial interactions, and it is especially difficult for a child to decipher the true significance of these unfinished phrases. One thing the young girl notices, nonetheless, is that full sentences can be spoken when it is a question of her brother, and she attributes this sudden coherence to the presence of this "masculine element": "Phew! I got a normally constructed sentence, grammatically speaking." Strikingly enough, the "social, moral, and cultural realities" that are eventually communicated in more complicated "causal expressions" as the protagonist gets older will come to bear on her personal parenting dilemma when her own daughter asks for permission to go out, as the suggestive ending to this short story puts forth.

The ninth short story's title, "Night and Silence," recalls *Nuit et brouillard* by the French filmmaker Alain Resnais, an inventive cinematic documentary on the Second World War, another reference to this major conflict that provides an important point of comparison, as well as a point of reference that facilitates productive contemplation in Maïssa Bey's oeuvre. The short story contains a startling account of a defenseless teenager's ordeal in an Islamic militant camp during the civil war in Algeria. The fifteen-year-old victim of repeated rape at the hands of Islamists has become pregnant and is being held captive in another setting until the baby's birth. Through a first-person narrative voice, this adolescent is able to pick her own words to tell of her trials in a time when many woman and girls are being punished heavily for a crime so seemingly inoffensive as failing to wear the Muslim veil. The result of allowing this young person to express herself in this short story is a powerful, straightforward condemnation of the circumstances surrounding her treatment on all levels. Like the woman in the third short story, "In Good Faith upon My Honor," this teenager is aware of the fact that she is not the first to go through something like this, and she brings up the difficulty her mother knew with her multiple pregnancies. But the even greater intensity of her personal struggle is illuminated in commentary that reveals how certain verbal expressions can communicate painful situations obliquely. In contrast to her own subtle use of language, she uncovers the blatant misuse of sacred words by the Islamic militants who defiled her again and again; in the aftermath of these violations she claims that she "can no longer say those words," that she can no longer invoke God as these men did before every move, even acts of rape, punishment, and murder. She hints that those who have hurt her will not be held responsible for these actions, indicating instead that if her father and brothers were still alive, they would have to kill her in order "not to have to face the dishonor" of the "sin that [she] didn't commit" but whose consequences she must bear, in shame. Her story leaves the reader hanging, in a sense, because her fate and her future remain up in the air.

"On a Comma," the sixth short story, calls attention in its very title to punctuation, a topic that is not anecdotal, since such signs as ellipses and question marks can influence the meanings of the words around them. Indeed, "On a Comma" refers to the inconclusive story that is told within another tale, thanks to a discovered diary that was presumably left behind when its author was forced to leave her home in a hurry. It appears that this precipitous departure was part of an exchange of one family for another in 1962, toward the end of the Algerian War, and eighteen-year-old Marie's notebook remained when she and her loved ones left the neighborhood where they lived among other *pied-noir* inhabitants of Algeria. Sarah is consumed by her reading in 1992 of this personal text which dates back thirty years, especially since she is the same age as the author of this text when she composed it. Her fascination with the written words of the previous occupant of her home is intensified by the fact that the earlier war that determines Marie's daily life finds an echo in Sarah's everyday experience during the civil war that racks the streets of the Algiers she knows, "a present" that she presumes is as "terrible" as Marie's "youth had been." The two major conflicts are brought together in powerful ways through the superposition of the expressions of these two young women from different ethnicities and religions who are nonetheless both at a pivotal age, on the verge of becoming adults, filled with similar concerns regarding interpersonal relationships and future goals, amid the uncertainty of war.

The short story "On a Comma" has a particularly strong impact because of the alternating prose that allows each of the protagonists to express her quotidian existence in the same location, in a different time that is nonetheless marked by similarly harrowing circumstances. Sarah's reflections on Marie's prose allow the author to make a statement on the possibility of the act of writing to relate realities, to provide unprecedented access to the lives of others, as well as to preserve the past from oblivion, providing "history with a human face": "when I take up the notebook, when at night I listen to her voice which runs all the way along these pages yellowed in the shade of time and forgetfulness, in these words written with purple ink, it's as if Marie were here, beside me." Writing can cut across space and time, providing company and assuring that, like Sarah, readers of any text may feel that they are "no longer alone." When the gestures of writing and reading are truly effective, they reach over "the disfigured town, divided by hatred and despair," embodying hope for reconciliation between "European" and "Muslim" families that is not limited to an exchange of one domestic location for another but that transcends geographical demarcations and racial designations.

As this collection of short stories demonstrates so well, Maïssa Bey is especially attentive to words, measuring their import and reflecting on their usage in explicit ways within the literary work. This intense appreciation for the manner in which certain syllables can wield an influence on not only our thoughts but also our actions, and can truly come to shape our perception of all that surrounds us, is a distinguishing aspect of her writing. If Bey has a way with words, it is in large part because she weighs her words with such care, conscientiously considering all expressions according to etymology and impact in texts that often call attention to the ways words enter into our consciousness without our awareness. And yet, even though she recognizes their immense power, Bey does not place too much stock in words. This is why she allows silence and suggestion to come through in her literary creations, in an attempt to communicate those aspects of existence which can only be alluded to, or which ultimately elide words entirely. Some experiences and emotions are unspeakable, and yet they can be hinted at, conveyed through a subtle turn of phrase, or even through a simple phrase from a song.

Lyrical Intimations: Refrains Running throughout Maïssa Bey's Oeuvre

The first of the eleven short stories that comprise the collection *Sous le jasmin la nuit* is the eponymous tale translated as "Under the Jasmine at Night." This italicized title appears within the text itself, inserted twice into a long sentence reflecting on the spontaneity with which these words have come to the mind of the woman at the center of this story. What this repetition of the title creates, placed as it is among juxtaposed short sentences that defy grammar, is the altogether appropriate sensation of a refrain. This title refers to a well-known love song in Arabic, "That el Yasmina Fellil," by the twentieth-century Tunisian composer Hédi Jouini. It is a musical creation with revolutionary implications, even if the character who permits its words to gently traverse her lips isn't too careful to distinguish among the syllables, to articulate its amorous words. This indication that the song has arrived without warning or forethought, and that it has entered Maya's being and somehow touched her, provides some insight into the way words *speak us,* even if they are not always reflected upon. Of course, verses from poems and songs can slip into our consciousness in very specific ways.

This is not Bey's only publication to bear a title that is a quotation from a piece of music with political overtones. Another example can be found in the 2014 play *Chaque pas que fait le soleil,* in which the female protagonist settles upon this title taken from the French poet Paul Valéry in a touching theatrical exploration of the intense potential of words and the threat they represent to those who wish to stifle freedom of thought and expression. The 2015 novel *Hizya* is inspired by another poem, this one composed by the nineteenth-century Algerian poet Mohamed Ben Guitton, that is also a song described in detail in the work of fiction.

It is crucial to note that the title of *Do You Hear in the Mountains* ... recalls a verse from "La Marseillaise," the French national anthem, the entire line of which is quoted correctly within the narrative. On the book's cover, however, the text has been modified to read *"montagnes"* rather than *"campagnes,"* a word so similar that it almost slips by without notice but that nonetheless deserves attention because it represents a significant shift in emphasis; it is no longer a landscape of French fields but rather the mountainous terrain of Algeria that is evoked in this transposition. This lexical change also harks back to one of the most renowned songs of the Algerian War, "Min Jibalina," whose lyrics in the original Arabic open with the message that the shouts of free men calling others to independence come "from our mountains." Another song is cited in *Do You Hear in the Mountains* ... , the tune called the "Chant des Africains." Written at the beginning of World War I to honor the bravery of a Moroccan regiment fighting for France, it was modified in World War II to acknowledge the Africans who fought with the Allies and was then adopted by the *pied-noir* community during the Algerian War. The history of this song serves as a reminder in this text that songs can come back and be used again, inflected differently, with alterations to lyrics that modify their messages in important ways. In the context of the train ride across France, the former French soldier hears echoes of these lyrics as they intermingle with others: "Snippets of songs stuck like burrs in the innermost recesses of consciousness." These resonant phrases and refrains take their place deep in the minds of those who have heard them, whatever the circumstances. Their power to remain, when other memories fade, is what gives such lyrics a prominent role among the abundant quoted references that grace the pages of Bey's written works.

Pairing Up: Fleshing Out the Figure of the Father

The penultimate short story in *Under the Jasmine at Night* carries a title that is at once a quotation and a question, "What's an Arab?" In this probing text, Maïssa Bey once again adopts the technique of alternating roman and italicized type in order to convey more than one point of view. The italicized portion of this story is accorded to the first-person voice of the adult narrator, who reflects on her textual choices as she attempts to render moments from her childhood in written form. The print in roman type reveals episodes from her early life in vivid third-person prose. The eponymous inquiry is pronounced by a precocious girl who represents the narrator in her younger years, and while the narrator doesn't remember the response she received, she does remember her vague impressions at the time: "Still the word makes images jump out."

This tenth short story in the collection *Under the Jasmine at Night* is an autobiographically inspired piece in which the author stages her own grasping at the hazy reminiscences of this period that preceded her father's death. The educated older self attributes to her earlier incarnation a sentiment that she would not have known how to articulate at the time: "There is also this word that imposes itself with such strength that it makes me throw out all the others: humiliation. First humiliation. So strong, so unacceptable that it determined all the rest. My life. But this word is too difficult to be thought of by a child. Too heavy. The first experience of injustice seems more adequate to me." The child's question, which might have been prompted by a comment directed at her, perhaps in the French school that she attended thanks to her father's role as a teacher there, recalls the ringing accusation from *Do You Hear in the Mountains* . . . that the woman in the train called out: "Arabs, I'm sure! I saw them!" In that text, the narrative voice takes a moment to ponder the usefulness of "classifications" in order to "situate someone" before honing in on the seemingly excessive number of terms that have been invented by the French for this group of people, ranging from designations such as "Muslim Frenchmen from Algeria" to the blanket use of the first name Fatma to refer to all women without distinguishing among them. Most of these expressions for those from Algeria were "insulting, racist terms," whereas the French were not the victims of a similar profusion of incendiary words.

In response to the question "What's an Arab?," the girl's father makes her aware of a whole lexicon, unloading loaded terms one after the other: "War. Enemies. French. Arabs. Liberation." For a child as young as she is, these are revelatory expressions that tell of a world she had not imagined could be so fraught: "He talks. She listens. Avidly. She grasps the words, captures them, forever." Not much later, when their home is invaded by French soldiers, other expressions can be added to the list, words that are powerful enough that they enable these men to take her father away without any proof of his guilt: "Network, cell, *fellaga.*"

The immense importance of official terms in times of war comes across with such strength in *Do You Hear in the Mountains* . . . when it becomes evident that the character named Jean has not forgotten the expressions that were impressed upon him when he was a young soldier in Algeria: "maintaining order," "pacification," "our mission," "refusal to collaborate," and "crush the rebellion" are among "the words" "still imprinted in his memory" forty years later. In order to push their dialogue to include the words that ultimately described her father's demise, the woman in the train reminds this French veteran that formulations like "firewood duty" allowed unthinkable acts to be carried out without acknowledgment, making the crucial point that euphemisms somehow smoothed over such crimes as torture and execution.

The reflective narration in "What's An Arab?" indicates that following the father's forcible removal from the home on that fateful February night in 1957, the list of heavy terms becomes even longer: "Still other words: torture, execution, death. And still later on, martyr." But what weighs the narrator down most dramatically is a different word: "absence." The mother who takes in the news of her husband's demise does not have recourse to discursive speech but instead lets out a "cry," followed by "howls" and "curses," in a reaction that recalls other outbursts that punctuate other short stories in this collection. The summary executions of her father and uncles meant that the young inquiring girl subsequently fled for her life, along with her mother and siblings.

This tragic set of events can never be rectified. The lives that were wrongly taken can never be restored. But if the father's body lies in an anonymous mass grave, the literary endeavors of his daughter have nonetheless served to preserve the name of Yagoub Benameur for posterity. And if there are only a few tangible remnants from his life, those documents and images are also respected and retained on the printed page in *Do You Hear in the Mountains* ... For even if her memories are misty, all is clearly not lost from Maïssa Bey's early exposure to her father. In fact, as she reveals in *Do You Hear in the Mountains* ... and "What's An Arab?," two complementary texts that combine to form a composite image of this paternal figure, he was *the* indispensable influence, forming and informing her for a career in writing. This is how the narrator expresses it in "What's An Arab?": "To retrieve my father's words now. I immediately perceive their softness, the desire to convince me by looking for the right words. His words ... anchored in me. Forever." She has paid him back in inexpressibly significant ways, for all the notes of her formidable oeuvre come together to sing his praise.

BIBLIOGRAPHY

Works by Maïssa Bey
(in chronological order)

Au commencement était la mer. Paris: Marsa, 1996.

A contre-silence. Suivi d'un choix de textes: Entretien avec Martine Marzloff. Grigny: Editions Paroles d'Aube, 1998.

Nouvelles d'Algérie. Paris: Grasset, 1998.

Cette fille-là. La Tour d'Aigue: Editions de l'Aube, 2001.

Entendez-vous dans les montagnes. . . . La Tour d'Aigue: Editions de l'Aube/ Algiers: Editions Barzakh, 2002.

L'ombre d'un homme qui marche au soleil: Réflexions sur Albert Camus. Montpellier: Editions Chèvre-feuille étoilée, 2004.

Sous le jasmin la nuit. La Tour d'Aigue: Editions de l'Aube, 2004.

"Lalla." In *Des Nouvelles d'Algérie 1974–2004,* edited by Christiane Chaulet-Achour. Paris: Éditions Métailié, 2005.

Sahara, mon amour. La Tour d'Aigue: Editions de l'Aube, 2005.

Above All, Don't Look Back. Translated by Senja L. Djelouah. Charlottes-ville: University of Virginia Press, 2009. First published as *Surtout ne te retourne pas.* La Tour d'Aigue: Editions de l'Aube, 2005.

Bleu blanc vert. La Tour d'Aigue: Editions de l'Aube, 2006.

"Fragments." In *Mon père,* edited by Leïla Sebbar, 65–74. Montpellier: Editions Chèvre-feuille étoilée, 2007.

"França?" In *C'était leur France: En Algérie, avant l'Indépendance,* edited by Leïla Sebbar, 53–65. Paris: Gallimard, 2007.

"My Father, the Rebel." Translated by Suzanne Ruta. *World Literature To-day,* November 2007, 27–30. First published in 1998 as "Mon père, ce rebelle," in *A contre-silence,* 80–90.

Pierre sang papier ou cendre. La Tour d'Aigue: Editions de l'Aube, 2008.

L'une et l'autre. La Tour d'Aigue: Editions de l'Aube, 2009.

Puisque mon cœur est mort. La Tour d'Aigue: Editions de l'Aube/Algiers: Editions Barzakh, 2010.

Tu vois c'que j'veux dire. Montpellier: Editions Chèvre-feuille étoilée, 2013.

Chaque pas que fait le soleil. Montpellier: Editions Chèvre-feuille étoilée, 2014.

On dirait qu'elle danse. Montpellier: Editions Chèvre-feuille étoilée, 2014.
Hizya. La Tour d'Aigue: Editions de l'Aube, 2015.

Scholarly Articles and Books on Maïssa Bey

Achille, Etienne. "Des Arabes, j'en suis sûre!" Rompre le silence dans *Entendez-vous dans les montagnes* . . . de Maïssa Bey." *French Forum* 38, no. 1–2 (Winter/Spring 2013): 251–65.

Belkaid, Meryem. "Writing beyond Trauma: Assia Djebar, Maïssa Bey, and New National Identities after Algeria's Civil War." *Journal of North African Studies* 23, no. 1–2 (2018): 125–39.

Belkous, Meriem. *Lui/Elle: Deux voix algériennes au pluriel. Étude critique sur l'Histoire et la polyphonie dans "Bleu blanc vert" de Maïssa Bey.* Paris: Études universitaires européennes, 2017.

Carlson, Anne F. "From Orality to Reading in Maïssa Bey's *Bleu Blanc Vert.* "Transgression, Imagination and Self-Assertion." Special issue, *Women in French Studies* (2012): 265–82.

Chaulet-Achour, Christiane. "Écrire en Algérie: Maïssa Bey, sept années de creation." *Notre Librairie* 150 (April–June 2003): 76–80.

———. "Maïssa Bey: L'épreuve de la mémoire," *Algérie Littérature/Action* 63–64 (September–October 2002): 59–62.

Farhoud, Samira, and Carey Watt. "'Encounters' of Frustration and Hope in the Writing of Maïssa Bey." In *Algeria Revisited: History, Culture, Identity,* edited by Rabah Aissaoui and Claire Eldridge, 135–54. London: Bloomsbury, 2017.

Julien, Hélène M. "L'art de la fugue: Identité, espace et narration dans *Shérazade* de Leïla Sebbar et *Cette fille-là* de Maïssa Bey." *French Review* 90, no. 2 (December 2016): 76–87.

Kerboubi, Leila. "Les stratégies énonciatives dans *Entendez-vous dans les montagnes* . . . de Maïssa Bey: L'écriture impersonnelle." *Synergies Algérie* 16 (2012): 59–65.

McIlvanney, Siobhán. "Fictionalising the Father in Maïssa Bey's *Entendez-vous dans les montagnes* . . ." *Hawwa, Journal of Women of the Middle East and the Islamic World* 12 (2014): 195–220.

———. "Fighting for Independence: Leïla Marouane's *La jeune fille et la mère* and Maïssa Bey's *Cette fille-là.*" *Experiment and Experience: Women's Writing in France 2000–2010,* edited by Gill Rye and Amaleena Damlé, 59–74. Oxford: Peter Lang, 2013.

Mehta, Brinda J. *Dissident Voices of Arab Women: Voices against Violence.* New York: Routledge, 2014.

———. "Fractured Silences and Youth Dystopia in Maïssa Bey's Theatrical Writings." *International Journal of Francophone Studies* 19, no. 3–4 (2016): 253–74.

Mortimer, Mimi. Afterword to *Above All, Don't Look Back*, by Maïssa Bey, translated by Senja L. Djelouah. Charlottesville: University of Virginia Press, 2009.

Orlando, Valérie K. *The Algerian New Novel: The Poetics of a Modern Nation, 1950–1979*. Charlottesville: University of Virginia Press, 2017.

Rice, Alison. *Polygraphies: Francophone Women Writing Algeria*. Charlottesville: University of Virginia Press, 2012.

Rosello, Mireille. "Comment s'inventer un père écrivain: Albert Camus chez Maïssa Bey." *Expressions maghrébines* 14, no. 1 (2015): 7–21.

Segarra, Marta. *Nouvelles romancières du Maghreb*. Paris: Karthala, 2010.

Soler, Ana. "*Bleu blanc vert* de Maïssa Bey: Regards croisés sur trois décennies d'indépendance algérienne." *Nouvelles Études Francophones* 24, no. 1 (2009): 143–56.

———. "La parole au féminin: La narratrice de *Cette fille-là* de Maïssa Bey." *Présence Francophone* 70 (2003): 169–83.

Valat, Colette. "Maïssa Bey: L'écriture de la révolte." In *Horizons Maghrébins: Le droit à la mémoire: Littératures féminines francophones, avec et autour de Maïssa Bey*, 11–32. Toulouse: Presses Universitaires du Mirail, 2009.

Intertextual References and Complementary Texts

Bey, Maïssa. Interview for the journal *Binatna*, 6 July 2017. Accessed on the website of the French embassy in Algiers: https://dz.ambafrance.org/Entretien-avec-l-ecrivaine-Maissa-Bey-pour-la-revue-Binatna.

Calvino, Italo. *Se une notte d'inverno un viaggiatore*. Turin: Giulio Einaudi Editore, 1979. Translated by Martin Rueff as *Si une nuit d'hiver un voyageur*. Paris: Seuil, 1981. Translated by William Weaver as *If on a Winter's Night a Traveler*. New York: Harcourt Brace, 1981.

Djebar, Assia. *L'Amour, la fantasia*. Paris: J.-C. Lattès, 1985; Albin Michel, 1995. Translated by Dorothy S. Blair as *Fantasia: An Algerian Cavalcade*. Portsmouth, NH: Heinemann, 1993.

Resnais, Alain. *Nuit et brouillard*. Translated as *Night and Fog*. Paris: Argos Films, 1956.

Sartre, Jean-Paul. *Huis clos*. Paris: Gallimard, 1947. Translated by Paul Bowles as *No Exit*. New York: Samuel French, 1958.

Schlink, Bernhard. *Der Vorleser*. Zurich: Diogenes, 1995. Translated by Bernard Lortholary as *Le liseur*. Paris: Gallimard, 1996. Translated by Carol Brown Janeway as *The Reader*. New York: Random House, 1997.

Valéry, Paul. *"Mon Faust" (Ébauches)*. Paris: Gallimard, 1946.